Counter-terrorism: Containment and Beyond

Jonathan Stevenson

ADELPHI PAPER 367

Oxford University Press, Great Clarendon Street, Oxford OX2 6DP
Oxford New York

Athens Auckland Bangkok Bombay Calcutta Cape Town
Dar es Salaam Delhi Florence Hong Kong Istanbul Karachi
Kuala Lumpur Madras Madrid Melbourne Mexico City Nairobi
Paris Taipei Tokyo Toronto
and associated companies in Ibadan

Oxford is a trade mark of Oxford University Press

Published in the United States
by Oxford University Press Inc., New York

© The International Institute for Strategic Studies 2004

First published October 2004 by **Oxford University Press** for
The International Institute for Strategic Studies
Arundel House, 13–15 Arundel Street, Temple Place, London WC2R 3DX
www.iiss.org

Director John Chipman
Editor Tim Huxley
Copy Editor Jill Dobson
Production Simon Nevitt

British Library Cataloguing in Publication Data
Data available

Library of Congress Cataloguing in Publication Data

ISBN 0-19-856759-6
ISSN 0567-932x

Contents

Glossary

CBRN	chemical, biological, radiological, nuclear
CFR	Council on Foreign Relations
CIA	Central Intelligence Agency
C-TPAT	Customs-Trade Partnership Against Terrorism
CSI	Container Security Initiative
CTR	Cooperative Threat Reduction programme
DARPA	Defense Advanced Research Project Agency
DCI	Director of Central Intelligence
DHS	Department of Homeland Security
ETA	Euskadi ta Askatasuna
Eurodac	European Automated Fingerprints Identification System
FAA	Federal Aviation Administration
FATF	Financial Aid Task Force
FBI	Federal Investigation Bureau
FISA	Foreign Intelligence Surveillance Act
FSF	Financial Stability Forum (G7)
FTO	foreign terrorist organisation
GCHQ	Government Communications Headquarters
GIA	Armed Islamic Group
IIRO	Islamic International Relief Organisation
INS	Immigration and Naturalization Service
IMO	International Maritime Organisation
ISI	Inter-Services Intelligence directorate (Pakistan)
JCLEC	Jakarta Centre for Law Enforcement Cooperation
JDP	Justice and Development Party (Turkey)
JI	Jemaah Islamiah
JTAC	Joint Terrorism Analysis Centre (UK)
MANPADS	man-portable air defence system
MATRIX	Multistate Anti-Terrorism Information Exchange
MCA	Millennium Challenge Account
MILF	Moro Islamic Liberation Front
NEPAD	New Partnership for Africa's Development
NSPD	National Security Presidential Directive
NU	Nahdlatul Ulama (Indonesia)
PLO	Palestine Liberation Organisation
PSI	Proliferation Security Initiative
SIS	Schengen Information System
TIA	Total Information Awareness
TTIC	Terrorist Threat Integration Center
UAV	unmanned aerial vehicle
WMD	weapons of mass destruction

Introduction

The 11 September attacks revealed that the transnational terrorist threat facing the US and its partners was far more dangerous than most had previously discerned. It was now inarguable that al-Qaeda's leadership intended and could threaten to diminish the West's – and particularly the United States' – global political and military leverage, and ultimately to shift the balance of power from the West to Islam after a violent global confrontation. In that sense, the new terrorist threat is strategic, and it has spurred a worldwide mobilisation of intellectual and material resources comparable to that required by a world war. The analytic contours of counter-terrorism, however, have not changed. Prior to 11 September 2001, Paul R. Pillar, former deputy chief of the Counterterrorism Center at the Central Intelligence Agency (CIA) did not regard transnational Islamist terrorism as a strategic threat.[1] Nevertheless, he delineated four apt counter-terrorism parameters:

> *The major fronts on which the problem of terrorism can be addressed are the root conditions and issues that give rise to terrorist groups in the first place and motivate individuals to join them; the ability of such groups to conduct terrorist attacks; the intentions of groups regarding whether to launch terrorist attacks; and the defenses erected against such attacks.*[2]

None of these 'fronts' is inherently military. In fact, in the past states have generally chosen to downplay or minimise military responses to terrorist campaigns.[3] In Northern Ireland, for example, despite an initially military reaction and a continuing army presence, the British government accorded primary counter-terrorist authority to the civilian police very early in the conflict (1976) and treated republican and loyalist terrorism as essentially a law-enforcement problem and terrorists as criminals. This approach has produced qualified success.[4] Even against the singularly recalcitrant Basque terrorists of Euskadi ta Askatasuna, the Spanish government has resolutely used a criminalisation approach. American persistence in bringing to justice the Libyan-backed terrorists who blew up Pan Am Flight 103 over Lockerbie, Scotland, in 1988 appears to have helped incline Muammar Gaddafi towards opting out of the international terrorism business.[5]

Al-Qaeda and counter-terrorism

In the rare conflicts involving terrorism that have become militarised, such as those in Sri Lanka or south Lebanon, the terrorist group in question has also manifested the characteristics of a formal military force – in particular, the capacity to take and hold territory. Before and immediately after 11 September, al-Qaeda had effective dominion over Afghanistan through its religiously beholden landlord, the Taliban, and therefore appeared to qualify as such an exceptional group. And indeed, military action led by the United States against al-Qaeda and the Taliban swiftly occurred. In the wake of that action, some observers anticipated major coalition military intervention against a number of states deemed potential al-Qaeda hosts or collaborators. The speculative array of targets has included, at various times, Georgia, Indonesia, the Philippines, Somalia, Sudan and Yemen.

Yet no major action against these targets has occurred. It is true, of course, that US-led intervention in Iraq in 2003 had a counter-terrorism dimension and partial justification – namely, to deprive al-Qaeda of a potential state supplier of weapons of mass destruction (WMD). But certainly in retrospect, and to some extent prospectively as well, the intervention was more centrally premised not on any tactical counter-terrorism goals but rather on the strategic objective of changing the political status quo in the Gulf and prompting political reform in the region that would diminish Islamist radicalism.

In areas where law-enforcement coverage is geographically, politically or institutionally limited – such as Southeast Asia and parts of the Persian Gulf – small military units may, by default, be required to meet everyday counter-terrorism needs and special regional demands such as that for maritime interdiction of terrorism-related piracy in Southeast Asia. In the Philippines, for instance, the US is providing tactical military assistance to the government in its effort to suppress Abu Sayyaf and the Moro Islamic Liberation Front, both al-Qaeda affiliates. The Pentagon's Regional Maritime Security Initiative (RMSI) may involve US Marines and special forces deployed on high-speed vessels to prevent and respond to seaborne terrorist operations in Southeast Asia. The Five-Power Defence Arrangements (involving Australia, Malaysia, New Zealand, Singapore and the United Kingdom) and Indonesia, Malaysia and Singapore trilaterally, began in late 2004 to move towards coordinated maritime counter-terrorism. The US is also furnishing military training and equipment to Georgia and Yemen in aid of counter-terrorism and maintaining a preventive and deterrent military presence in the Arabian Sea and Djibouti, and providing train-and-equip programmes for the security forces of Chad, Mali, Mauritania and Niger under the Pan Sahel Initiative. The CIA used a high-tech military asset, a *Predator* unmanned aerial vehicle mounted with *Hellfire* antitank missiles, to kill six al-Qaeda operatives travelling by car along a remote desert road in Yemen in November 2002. Navies and coast guards will be required to maintain maritime security against both terrorist attacks and terrorism-linked piracy, and to interdict ships suspected of carrying illicit WMD-related cargo under the Proliferation Security Initiative (PSI).

Yet deeper and more aggressive military commitments are unlikely, and there probably will be little opportunity for targeted killings. The al-Qaeda network's very strength lies in its non-military nature: its clandestine character; the transnational dispersal of personnel; the organisational 'flatness' of its network; its decentralised command-and-control; and its reliance on asymmetric threats. Further, al-Qaeda's radical Islamic vocation indicates a high resistance to intimidation by brute force, and raises the possibility that the group might actually welcome ostentatious applications of force by its state and coalition adversaries as a means of radicalising the *umma* – that is, the totality of the world's Muslims.

Unlike, say, the Provisional Irish Republican Army (IRA)'s goal of a united Ireland, al-Qaeda's maximalist political agenda does not easily admit of any amenability to diplomacy or negotiation. Correspondingly, the group, in contrast to the IRA, has little real interest in overt political bargaining. Al-Qaeda – which means 'the base' in Arabic – is a global jihadist movement with several related revolutionary objectives. The movement's priorities are not always clear from its public rhetoric. Al-Qaeda leader Osama bin Laden has cited the US military presence in Saudi Arabia and American support for Israel in the Israeli–Palestinian conflict as justifications for al-Qaeda terrorist operations. More obscurely but nevertheless tellingly, however, he has referred to the alleged historical humiliation of Islam at the hands of the Judeo-Christian West. Al-Qaeda leaders have cited Spain's expulsion of Muslims in the fifteenth century as a source of its enmity towards the West. Al-Qaeda spokesman Suleiman Abu Ghaith has said that there can be no truce until the group has killed four million Americans, whereupon others could convert to Islam.

From such pronouncements, three specific objectives can be inferred. First, al-Qaeda seeks to overthrow Arab regimes – in particular Egypt's and Saudi Arabia's, whose close relationships with the United States render them 'apostate' and thus inimical to true Islam. These are the 'near enemies'. Second, it wants to debilitate the US – al-Qaeda's prime 'far enemy' – as a superpower and purge Muslim states of all American and Western political, economic and cultural influences. Third, and less centrally, al-Qaeda would like to eliminate the state of Israel (another 'far enemy') and liberate the Palestinian people. None of these aims are realistically negotiable, and al-Qaeda's broader – but equally decipherable – goal of an apocalyptic 'clash of civilisations' between Islam and the Judeo-Christian West en route to a pan-Islamic caliphate merely underlines its implacability.[6] Thus, drawing down American military deployments in the Middle East/Gulf region and constructive US intervention in the Israeli-Palestinian conflict would not completely defuse the al-Qaeda leadership's anti-American and anti-Western wrath. Given al-Qaeda's stated means and ends, bin Laden's April 2004 offer of a truce to European partners in the counter-terrorism coalition on condition that they cease supporting US strategic initiatives in the Muslim world – summarily rejected – should be considered a psychological operation designed to intimidate them into diluting operational cooperation with and political support for the United States rather than a good-faith initiation of conflict resolution.

Accordingly, the effects of diplomacy on the 'new terrorism' seem destined to be attenuated and incremental and to enjoy relatively little enhancement by military threats or actions.

Nevertheless, the transnational Islamic terrorist threat can be usefully characterised as a global insurgency. Constructive parallels – if not direct analogies – can be drawn between past policies that have worked against 'old' ethno-nationalist terrorist groups and prospective policies for dealing with transnational Islamic terrorist groups despite their well-known and palpable differences. For instance, it is worth remembering that once the British government wedded enlightened social policies to vigorous law enforcement and intelligence operations, robust constitutional or 'soft' nationalism surpassed militant 'physical force' republicanism as a political influence in the Catholic community. An analogous development in Islam could not be expected to move al-Qaeda towards formal compromise as it did Sinn Fein and the IRA. But empowering moderate Islam in the larger Muslim community would perforce diminish al-Qaeda's constituency, its political strength and ultimately its operational efficacy. Likewise, although deterrence in the narrow sense of threatened retaliation will not work too well against jihadists, they may not be totally immune to such deterrence and certainly are not impervious to deterrence through the denial of their political objectives.[7] The fact that the global Islamist terrorist movement is essentially horizontal, multinational and heterogeneous means that it can be disaggregated into discrete components, which are liable to be susceptible to varying degrees of deterrent threats.

Of course, even during the Cold War, against a monolithic state-based adversary whose designs were simpler to determine and whose structural constraints were similar to those faced by Western states, it took decades for the West to refine deterrence and then move to rollback and victory. In the meantime, containment was required. In this connection, the broader notion of deterrence by denial of opportunity should become steadily more salient. It remains doubtful that the West's application of military power will play a central role. Confirming a strong consensus among counter-terrorism analysts, the 9/11 Commission Report, released in July 2004, found no institutional or planning-level links between al-Qaeda and Saddam Hussein's regime. Despite some jihadist involvement in the Iraq insurgency that arose in May 2003, terrorism in Iraq is mainly local, which negates any notion that the US occupation of Iraq has created a 'honey trap' into which jihadists will be lured and exposed in lieu of attacking the US itself or other Western targets. Despite the short-term importance of the Afghanistan intervention in limiting the al-Qaeda leadership's freedom of action, advances in the use of special forces and small units against unconventional adversaries, and the substantial preventive and deterrent presence the US military is maintaining in the Arabian Sea and Djibouti, armed counter-terrorist military operations are likely to be few and far between.

A year after the attacks on the World Trade Center and the Pentagon, following arrests of suspected al-Qaeda affiliates in Pakistan, Singapore and Buffalo, New York, US President George W. Bush acknowledged that al-Qaeda would have to be dismantled 'one person at a time'.[8] The lion's share of counter-terrorism against al-Qaeda's transnational terrorist threats therefore will be conducted on the law-enforcement and intelligence fronts. Operationally thwarting al-Qaeda most essentially requires the efficient application of finite non-military resources.[9] This task, in turn, calls for an unprecedented degree of transnational inter-agency coordination and cooperation. The day-to-day, largely civilian task of monitoring and suppressing terrorist activity is arguably the most crucial component of that effort.

The operational challenge

Al-Qaeda has brought into its fold substantial national or regional terrorist groups, such as Egyptian Islamic Jihad, which it formally and explicitly incorporated in 1998, and Indonesia-based Jemaah Islamiah. However, it is not a unitary hierarchical institution, but rather a loose and essentially horizontal affiliation of allied and sympathetic groups and individuals – often labelled a 'network of networks'. Nevertheless, al-Qaeda does have a governing council, or shura, headed by bin Laden, and could operate on its own – as it appeared to do in the case of the 11 September attacks. It also has considerable financial resources, which include bin Laden's personal wealth and contributions donated, through charitable fronts, by wealthy, religiously conservative Arabs – substantially from Saudi Arabia. The group's cells operate semi-autonomously, maintaining links through field commanders to bin Laden and the shura, who can activate networks and give operational orders. These factors permit the organisation to blend seamlessly into societies in ways that are not easily detectable and therefore are relatively unsusceptible to the use of military force – to achieve, in a word, 'virtuality'. While *Operation Enduring Freedom* was the keynote of the US-led post-11 September counter-terrorism campaign, and has hobbled al-Qaeda's capacity for mass-casualty attack, it has also accelerated its drive towards virtuality. The expulsion of the Taliban and al-Qaeda from Afghanistan impelled an already highly decentralised and elusive transnational terrorist network to become even more virtual and protean and therefore even harder to identify and neutralise.[10] Although many local or regional jihadist groups suspected of involvement in post-11 September operations may have no direct operational links to al-Qaeda, it still acts as their common ideological and logistical hub. Bin Laden's charisma, presumed survival and elusiveness enhance the organisation's iconic power. Furthermore, al-Qaeda can offer financial, planning and procurement assistance.

If Afghanistan was once a 'terrorist-sponsored state', al-Qaeda now has no state to defend, which affords it maximum freedom of movement and minimises its need for dedicated 'bricks-and-mortar' physical infrastructure. Al-Qaeda operatives are thus able to 'hide in plain sight'. Al-Qaeda or its protégés are present in over 60 countries. Intelligence agencies estimate that at least 20,000 jihadists were trained in its Afghanistan camps between 1996 and late 2001. Only a fraction of that number have been killed or captured since 11 September, and most jihadist operations after 11 September have involved al-Qaeda cells or affiliates that have coalesced around, or at least drawn from, training camp alumni. Moreover, recruitment has continued – probably at higher levels, at least subsequent to the Iraq intervention, than before the 11 September attacks. Post-11 September investigations have also revealed al-Qaeda's high aptitude for improvisation in tradecraft and for eluding official scrutiny. For example, Mounir el-Motassadeq, an al-Qaeda member specifically designated not to participate in the 11 September attacks, signed legal documents in the names of active terrorists in the Hamburg cell run by suspected 11 September ringleader Muhammad Atta, so that they appeared to be in Germany when in fact they were in the US.

Al-Qaeda members have limited their use of electronically traceable telecommunications equipment – such as cell phones, satellite phones and the internet – to hinder detection by technical means.[11] Yet, while electronic communications are indispensable, they are also capable of mastering more sophisticated encryption techniques. Noted one former US counter-terrorism official: 'On the whole, they're better off without Afghanistan. They now have total global mobility'.[12] Post-Afghanistan, al-Qaeda remains a terrorist 'network of networks' with unequalled global leverage. Rather than the holding company to which it was often likened before and immediately after 11 September, al-Qaeda has become more like a dominant multinational full-service investment bank – available to serve any number of sympathetic terrorist groups or insurgencies.

Argument in brief

Al-Qaeda is a resilient organisation with a religiously turbo-charged maximalist agenda; it will not go quietly. The US-led counter-terrorism coalition will need an integrated containment strategy that incorporates military, intelligence, law-enforcement, diplomatic and economic measures. In the short term, the United States' reaction to 11 September has been, appropriately, to decrease vulnerabilities by bolstering homeland security, denying al-Qaeda access to co-optable states and regions and to weapons of mass destruction, killing and arresting terrorists, and developing a horizontal, multi-national law-enforcement and intelligence network to better cope with al-Qaeda's virtuality and its standing threat. American officials believe that at least half a dozen terrorist plots were thwarted during the year subsequent to the 11 September attacks. Not all vulnerabilities can be plugged, however. Accordingly, long-term political and economic diplomacy will be key to defeating al-Qaeda. But because its leadership's agenda is not negotiable, these instruments must aim to outflank rather than directly to tame al-Qaeda. The US and its partners will need to adopt proactive and coordinated policies to set the Israelis and the Palestinians on a path to accommodation, thus vitiating one of Bin Laden's central political pretexts. More broadly, through economic diplomacy and discreet pressure to democratise, they will have to convince untrusting and systematically misinformed Muslim populations that they can prosper without either destroying the West or relinquishing their traditions to Western cultural influences.

Chapter 1 of this paper will examine homeland security in the US and other countries, focusing on the necessity of 'forward' measures and multinational cooperation to secure national territory. Chapter 2 will look at the changes in intelligence and law-enforcement practices that the al-Qaeda threat has necessitated – in particular, inter-agency coordination and inter-governmental cooperation, and at the challenges presented by terrorist financing. Chapter 3 will explore what political and diplomatic agenda stands the best chance of marginalising al-Qaeda and its affiliates. The final chapter will sketch the structural and substantive requirements of a forward-looking, long-term counter-terrorism policy.

Chapter 1

Securing Territory Against Terrorists

When the World Trade Center and the Pentagon were attacked on 11 September 2001, the immediate perception of the American public was that the intelligence community had let them down. To an extent, this assessment was simplistic and unfair. Because intelligence, and therefore intelligence-based warnings, are inherently ambiguous, security premised on the threat assessments of intelligence agencies had no prospect of being sufficient protection against all terrorist operations. Accordingly, 11 September constituted a security failure writ large, involving not only intelligence inadequacies but also under-appreciated vulnerabilities in a wide range of areas including immigration, law enforcement and aviation security. At the same time, it became clear that the two most important federal agencies for gathering intelligence on transnational terrorist threats outside and inside the US – the CIA and the Federal Bureau of Investigation (FBI) – had, for both systemic and circumstantial reasons, failed to apprehend the saliency of al-Qaeda's threat. They also possessed or had access to disparate information before 11 September which could have prompted better preparedness had it been pooled, brought to the attention of high-level policymakers, or both.[1]

In March 2000, the presence of suspected terrorists and eventual hijackers Khalid al-Midhar and Nawaf al-Hazmi in the US was known by the CIA, but not communicated to the FBI until 23 August 2001. In spring and early summer 2001, the CIA had observed increased terrorist activity in the Persian Gulf and Europe. In July 2001, on the basis of his investigation of a Middle Eastern flight-school student who had contact with Abu Zubeida, a known major al-Qaeda figure, a special agent in the FBI's Phoenix field office had sent

a memorandum to headquarters in Washington recommending that
the Bureau investigate the possibility that Islamic terrorist suspects
were enrolling in flight schools. This was judged too costly in terms
of manpower, and the implied potential threat was never brought to
the attention of the White House. A 24 August 2001 CIA cable to the
Immigration and Naturalization Service (INS) warned that al-
Midhar and al-Hazmi should be put on the terrorist watch list.
Although the INS informed the CIA and the FBI that they had
already been admitted into the US and the FBI was unable to track
them down, neither the inter-agency Counter-terrorism Security
Group within the National Security Council nor the White House
itself was informed. They turned out to be two of the 11 September
hijackers. Also in August 2001, the FBI's Minneapolis field office
determined from French intelligence that Zacarias Moussaoui, who
had been arrested after seeking flight-simulator instruction, was an
Islamic extremist, but headquarters blocked the field office's
application for approval under the Foreign Intelligence Surveillance
Act (FISA) to examine his laptop computer, which would have
revealed his enrolment in a flight school that a known al-Qaeda
operative had also attended.[2] And on 10 September, the National
Security Agency had intercepted a highly ominous communication
between two Arabic speakers (one said that 'the match is about to
begin', the other that 'tomorrow is zero hour'); the intercept was not
translated until 12 September.

Even before the New York and Washington attacks, al-Qaeda
had hit or intended to hit soft targets overseas, but preferred targeting
American assets such as the US embassies in East Africa, an American
hotel in Jordan that serviced mainly Americans, the USS *Cole* in Aden,
and, in thwarted operations, the USS *The Sullivans*, US airliners
over the Pacific and the US embassies in Paris and Rome. After 11
September, al-Qaeda and its local followers expanded their target set
to include assets of Western allies and Christians or Jews of varied
provenance: the Australian, British and Israeli as well as the US
embassies in Singapore; Pakistani Christians; German tourists in
Tunisia; French submarine engineers in Pakistan; and the October
2002 bombing in Bali, Indonesia that killed 202 civilians, including
88 Australian tourists and a smaller number of Europeans and
Americans. In November 2002, in an audiotape believed to have
been made by Osama bin Laden, he expressly indicated that

Australia, Canada, France, Germany, Israel, Italy and the United Kingdom were targets. The Bali attack, and revelations that Jemaah Islamiah, al-Qaeda's local affiliate, also intended to target international schoolchildren in Indonesia, make it clear that al-Qaeda also regarded Southeast Asia as a particularly fertile 'field of jihad'.[3] The November 2002 al-Qaeda attacks on Israeli tourists in Kenya affirmed East Africa's place on the list.

Al-Qaeda's more flexible targeting is also doubtless a function of the group's loss of command-and-control and central planning capabilities as a result of the coalition's defeat of the Taliban, al-Qaeda's former hosts in Afghanistan. On one hand, it is now necessary for the group to exploit local affiliates to a greater extent than before. On the other hand, the group has fully metastasised. Unencumbered by a territorial base that would make a convenient cruise-missile target, al-Qaeda is now less susceptible to counter-terrorism measures than it was before 11 September. While it develops new angles of approach to mass-casualty terrorism in the US, and Palestinian terrorists (so far unconnected to al-Qaeda) draw blood in Israel, al-Qaeda can content itself that groups it supports or those that are inspired by its message or worldview can carry out high-payoff operations over a wider geographical range, exploiting countries with weak law-enforcement and intelligence institutions. A target is likely to be judged satisfactory as long as it fully symbolises the group's non-negotiable enmity to Christians, Jews and apostate Muslims.

US homeland security

After 11 September, the American view developed that threat assessment, proactive law enforcement and risk-management should be augmented by a replete range of standing measures to plug as many conceivable vulnerabilities as possible. Emblematic of this comprehensive approach is the United States' formal Homeland Security Advisory System, established by federal regulation in March 2002, which prescribes warnings at five different threat-condition levels corresponding to colours: low (green), guarded (blue), elevated (yellow), high (orange) and severe (red). Each level triggers an incrementally more stringent set of protective measures. The criteria for issuing the warning include the credibility of threat information; its degree of corroboration; specificity and imminence of the threat;

and gravity of potential consequences.[4] Establishing the standing capabilities required to neutralise threats, however, will take years, as the reorganisation of the American domestic architecture under a new Department of Homeland Security (DHS) constitutes the biggest restructuring of the federal bureaucracy since the implementation of the National Security Act of 1947. Further, though notable progress has been made since 11 September, the reorientation of the FBI from a strictly law-enforcement organisation to a more versatile counter-terrorism agency will require additional cultural and philosophical as well as operational adjustments.

Bureaucratic mission changes – even when accomplished – will not relieve the US law-enforcement and intelligence community of the need to maintain a constant state of alert and to pursue terrorist suspects aggressively. Within two months of 11 September, US authorities detained over 1,000 suspects and charged about 100 in connection with the investigation of the 11 September atrocities. The composition of that group provided an early sign of the difficulty of getting a grip on al-Qaeda. On 28 November 2001, US Attorney-General John Ashcroft released the names of 93 of the charged suspects, the specific charges brought against them and factual support for those charges. Only eleven suspects, whose names were withheld, were then considered to have connections to al-Qaeda. While most of the crimes with which they were charged were minor (e.g., illegal gun ownership, document fraud) and not intrinsically related to terrorism, each person did appear to have some connection – sometimes attenuated and possibly unwitting – to an illegal organisation.[5] For instance, Vicente Pierre, imprisoned on weapons charges, was linked to a New York-based radical Islamic group with Pakistani roots called al-Fuqra ('the impoverished' in Arabic). In turn, the FBI believes al-Fuqra is responsible for several bombings and murders, that some of its members were among *Wall Street Journal* reporter Daniel Pearl's killers and that it has links to al-Qaeda.[6] Kenys Galicia, a legal Salvadoran immigrant who worked as a secretary in a Falls Church, Virginia law office and for a fee falsely notarised documents that enabled several of the 11 September hijackers to obtain driver's licences, is arguably a more significant detainee precisely because of her ignorant venality. Her case shows how easy it was for a few Muslim terrorists on temporary visas to establish documentary credentials that facilitated their infiltration of American society.

It is equally significant that another 548 parties were being held only for immigration violations, premised ultimately on their ethnicity or national origin – in other words, non-US citizenship. Many were released soon after their arrest. Thus, the post-11 September law-enforcement experience in the US involved some 'overkill' with respect to non-citizens simply because there is more data available on them than on American citizens. By the same token, it is likely that fewer US citizens have been arrested than should have been. Federal authorities keep no records of foreign travel by US citizens and resident aliens. This is largely on account of the regulatory firewall erected between foreign and domestic intelligence in the 1990s, enshrined in FISA, which requires a showing of probable cause that a target of surveillance is merely a foreign agent (as opposed to a criminal) for judicial authorisation (i.e., a warrant) to conduct surveillance on a non-US citizen for intelligence-gathering purposes, but curtails the disclosure of any information thereby obtained to law-enforcement officers with arrest powers.

Small wonder, then, that as of early 2003 the US had captured only two 'American Taliban': John Walker Lindh and Yasser Esam Hamdi, who was born in Louisiana but spent most of his life in Saudi Arabia. Nine Americans had trained at the Haqqania Islamic religious boarding school, or madrassa, run by the Taliban and al-Qaeda in Pakistan's Northwest Frontier Province. Lindh received military instruction at a training camp in Pakistan run by Harakat al-Mujahideen and later at the al-Farooq camp in Afghanistan operated by al-Qaeda. As of April 2003, Lindh, Hamdi and would-be 'dirty' bomber José Padilla were the only arrested US citizens known to have trained in terrorist camps in Afghanistan or Pakistan. None of them appeared on official federal databases. A former FBI counter-terrorism agent estimated that between 1,000 and 2,000 aspiring jihadists departed the US for South Asia in the 1990s, and Pakistani authorities credited that estimate and added that about 400 recruits who trained in terrorist camps came from the US. Given that there are thousands of madrassas in Pakistan and Afghanistan and until *Operation Enduring Freedom* there were dozens of training camps in Afghanistan, it is a fair inference that more US citizens were radicalised in those places.[7] US law-enforcement officials note that there is no well-organised indigenous jihad movement in the US, and that many US-based jihadists fought for causes – like Chechen separatism or Muslim human rights in Bosnia – that were not intrinsically anti-American or global in scope. But given al-Qaeda's flexibility and improvisational flair, these observations are not directly apposite to assessing its overall threat. The point is that there are Muslims in the US of whom a significant number are likely to be ideologically aligned with al-Qaeda and therefore abjectly anti-American and presumptively dangerous.

In its post-Afghanistan mode, al-Qaeda could provide mere spiritual inspiration or actual operational assistance to such people – or both. The USA PATRIOT Act, passed in October 2001, substantially dismantles the regulatory barrier between domestic and foreign intelligence collection erected in the 1970s, expanding the range of information that FISA surveillance can cover and easing its dissemination among federal, state and local law-enforcement agencies. Due to political pressure from left-wing liberals and right-wing libertarians, the legislation was less intrusive than expected. The contents of e-mails, for instance, are still off-limits. While the USA PATRIOT Act has produced greater government access to more information about US citizens and non-citizens alike, the residual prohibitions on access to communications content and the notorious discrepancy between intelligence collection and processing capabilities has led the government towards some radical solutions. One of the more celebrated – and notorious – was the Defense Advanced Research Project Agency (DARPA)'s Total Information Awareness (TIA) research programme. The TIA programme aimed to cover a number of different areas. The most controversial one was geared to implementing state-of-the-art supercomputing and data-mining capabilities to enable the government to identify terrorists by detecting patterns of activity based on recorded information commercially or otherwise publicly recorded (travel, telecommunications, credit-card purchases, web-surfing, e-mail, etc.) and track their movements in near-real time.

TIA's framework for exploiting this transactional information came under heavy fire in Congress and from elements of the political left and right, on grounds that it would impermissibly infringe on individual privacy and civil liberties. Some degree of privacy protection, however, was built into the system. The computer programme employed would initially exclude names and other personal data from the transactions that it captured. If a suspicious transaction or series of transactions were detected, the names and personal details of those involved could be obtained only if a judge or other legal authority approved an application, by the intelligence analyst seeking that information, that showed sufficient justification for its disclosure. TIA would almost certainly have improved intelligence warning and counter-terrorism enforcement. But, even assuming a high degree of accuracy, anything less than 100% would also have meant numerous unwarranted invasions of privacy and a smaller number of unfair investigations and perhaps prosecutions. In January 2003, the Senate voted to halt the TIA programme, and the following September shut down DARPA's Information Awareness Office, which had developed the programme.

Although it is a virtual certainty that there are potential al-Qaeda-linked terrorists – both foreign and homegrown – on US soil, in the near-term the US probably will not be able to rely on leading-edge information technology to protect the American homeland. Thus, despite American declarations about putting in place a vulnerability-based system, the system that is actually evolving is only a very rough approximation thereof.[8] It appears to embody two de facto priorities, both involving 'forward' measures designed to push out the effective US border.

First, there are more stringent immigration controls to deny terrorists access to US territory. With increasingly incisive passenger profiling; better links among the databases of different law-enforcement agencies; strict federal registration requirements for males over 15, mainly from Muslim countries, on visitor, student or business visas; readier deportation of illegal immigrants; and closer monitoring of all foreign students on special visas, significant advances in filtering out those with terrorist intent have occurred. The DHS, which now has ultimate authority over who is issued a visa, in August 2003 quietly opened two law-enforcement offices in Saudi Arabia to investigate visa applicants suspected of links with al-Qaeda or affiliated groups. Other such offices are planned throughout the Muslim world.[9] The institution of these offices will presumably ease both the political and the administrative burden on State Department consular officers responsible for processing legitimate applications.

The US–Canada border is more porous than the southern, US–Mexico border, and remains of special concern. In an accord signed on 3 December 2001, the US agreed to integrate Canadian officials into its new Foreign Terrorist Tracking Task Force, to develop joint units to assess information on incoming passengers; and to increase immigration-control personnel assigned to Canada. US and Canadian multi-agency special law-enforcement teams to track terrorists and combat organised crime were also expanded. There are about 650,000 Muslims living in Canada, and they constitute a substantially higher proportion of the total population than they do in the US. American registration requirements have further impelled hundreds of illegal immigrants to the US to seek refuge in Canada by claiming asylum there. While Canada's refugee approval rate of 57% is only marginally higher than the United States' 54%, asylum applicants pending a decision on their applications are permitted to remain free in Canada but usually detained in the US.[10] Canadian police, despite being granted broader powers of preventive arrest after 11 September, have used them sparingly and are still more inclined to opt for surveillance over detention. This approach may be defensible. The Canadian Security Intelligence Service has said that it generates superior intelligence about al-Qaeda's modus operandi, which it shares with US authorities. But a surveillance-oriented approach to law enforcement makes sense only if complemented by a thoroughgoing and effective vulnerabilities-based approach to homeland security in general.[11]

The second priority is security in international commerce, to deny terrorists access to WMD and other implements that would facilitate mass-casualty attacks. Given the global sweep of the US economy – the volume of US international trade, in terms of dollars and containers, doubled between 1990 and 2001 and will double again between 2001 and 2005 – bilateral and multilateral cooperation in the implementation of forward measures is required to meet US homeland security needs. The US Coast Guard has established a 'Maritime Domain Awareness' programme, whereby agencies and private industry pool information on inbound ships, cargos, crews and passengers from multiple jurisdictions. Furthermore, Washington has enlisted the help of European, Asian and Middle Eastern trading partners to attain 'point-of-origin' cargo security. Under its Container Security Initiative (CSI), the US Customs Service is deploying specially trained officials at major ports worldwide to monitor shipping manifests and inspect cargo bound for the US, and will ultimately cover 70% of the 5.7 million containers shipped annually to the United States.[12]

Cooperation between the public and private sector on homeland security, based on a shared interest in preserving the flow of commerce, is also part of the US strategy. In April 2002, for example, seven large companies – Ford Motor Co., General Motors Co., DaimlerChrysler AG, BP America, Motorola Inc., Sara Lee Corp. and Target Corp. – initiated a charter risk-management programme, the Customs-Trade Partnership Against Terrorism (C-TPAT), whereby company shipments over the US–Canadian border are voluntarily subject to government-approved security procedures and supply data is provided in advance to the US Customs Service by computer in exchange for expedited 'fast track' treatment, aided by electronic transponders, for company trucks at the border. By August 2002, nearly 400 US companies had enrolled in C-TPAT. To secure 'fast track' treatment, the companies need to demonstrate better security practices at loading docks, ports and warehouses and allow the government to conduct background checks on shipping personnel and crews.

Shortfalls and solutions

There remain deficiencies with respect to tracking the movements of US citizens. It is not clear how salient their threat is. There is no doubt that al-Qaeda has a substantial presence in the US: as of February 2003, major arrests of those with suspected links to the group had been made in 17 states plus Washington DC. But few of those arrested have been found to be US citizens, fewer still to have trained in Afghanistan, and it is possible that al-Qaeda may be sceptical about the fidelity of non-Arabs or Arabs more likely to have been integrated into American society to a pan-Islamic, apocalyptically anti-American agenda. By the same token, however, their empirical scarcity may be precisely a product of poor intelligence, and al-Qaeda's demonstrated tactical ingenuity and flexibility suggests that a crackdown on non-citizens would heighten its interest in cultivating less scrutinised segments of the American population or criminally inclined immigrants, notably those from Latin America.[13]

Although continuing concerns about civil liberties may bar IT-based surveillance as extensive as TIA, a greater public appreciation of security needs appears likely to lead to better comprehensive tracking of the international movements of US citizens and resident aliens at lower cost. The DHS is implementing an expensive and admittedly controversial programme, US–VISIT, whereby a network of linked databases, coupled with biometric sensors, will enable immigration officials to establish the identity and recent security-relevant activities of visitors to the US immediately upon their application for entry – thus fashioning 'virtual borders' – and to track them once they are in the US.[14] Furthermore, an inclination on al-Qaeda's part to 'turn' US citizens would entail its crossing cultural boundaries and recruiting converts, like Padilla and Lindh, who need not be of Arab or Asian origin. This could present more promising opportunities to American intelligence and law-enforcement agencies to penetrate al-Qaeda. Better human intelligence in the domestic arena therefore may be one means by which US agencies compensate for the gaps in intelligence made unavoidable by the legal protections afforded American citizens.

Finally, efforts of technical focus comparable to the Manhattan Project may be warranted in several key defensive homeland-security areas. The first order of business would be to identify the full range of new threats. Some have already been pinpointed. While the Federal Aviation Administration (FAA) has been most concerned about collision avoidance between altitudes of 3,000 and 12,000 metres, terrorist attacks using cruise-missiles, UAVs or helicopters are most likely to occur beneath 3,000 metres, where a wider range of targets is proximate and detection by either North American Aerospace Defense Command or FAA radars becomes problematic.[15] Rapidly engineered vaccines against genetically manipulated pathogens are also needed, as are new capabilities for remote detection of radiological or fissile material, countermeasures against man-portable air defence systems (MANPADS) and bulk cargo screening. Work in all these areas is ongoing, but it is fragmented among agencies and in some instances, particularly MANPADS defence and cargo screening, under-funded in the president's FY2004 budget submission to Congress.[16] Overall, there has been a gap between the high hopes attending statutory and structural changes – reflected primarily in the creation of the DHS – and the funding and implementation of those changes. Although some shortfall was inevitable, a forward counter-terrorism strategy keyed to Iraq appears to have drawn resources and attention from homeland security.[17] The upshot is that American invulnerability remains only an aspiration.[18]

Transatlantic law-enforcement and intelligence cooperation

Europe was the key recruitment, planning and logistics base for the attacks on the World Trade Center and the Pentagon. After the 11 September attacks, the experience of France, Germany, Italy, Spain and the United Kingdom with serious terrorist threats over the past 30 years ensured European empathy with the United States' relatively fresh terrorist problem, alertness to the tactical utility to which al-Qaeda had put European hospitality and the robust cooperation of European countries with the US in pursuing and arresting terrorists. Between 11 September 2001 and February 2003, authorities in Belgium, Bosnia-Herzegovina, France, Germany, Italy, the Netherlands, Spain and the UK arrested over 200 suspected al-Qaeda terrorists. Over half were charged with terrorist offences. The pace of the arrests gathered momentum after the Bali and Kenya attacks and the November 2002 release of the tape in which bin Laden specifically mentioned four European countries as possible al-Qaeda targets. Through 2003, the majority of the suspects were North African, and the overwhelming majority of North Africans apprehended were Algerian. This suggested a more direct link to the Algeria-based Armed Islamic Group (GIA) – which conducted a terrorist campaign in France in the mid-1990s – than to al-Qaeda. But the GIA, having been marginalised in Algeria and known to harbour pan-Islamic ideals compatible with al-Qaeda's, would be a natural al-Qaeda ally. Significantly, the largest number of North Africans were arrested not in France but in the UK. This tends to confirm the trend observed among immediate post-11 September detainees in Europe: that most were likely to have became acclimatised to Western culture and perhaps alienated from it in France, but may have moved to Britain owing to its more acquiescent security regime and become radicalised and perhaps recruited there.

The no-warning Madrid bombings of 11 March 2004, which killed 191 people and have been traced to a largely Moroccan group with links to al-Qaeda, and the discovery of the chemical toxin ricin in UK raids in January 2003 raise an inference of mass-casualty intent on the part of terrorists operating in Europe. Thus, the heightened level of alert is likely to be durable. Europe clearly has a serious transnational Islamic terrorism problem.[19] Broadly speaking, liberal asylum laws and standards of religious and commercial freedom have made Europe an effective safe haven as well as a fundraising hub for aspiring terrorists.[20] Although several key European countries have more experience with terrorism on their soil than does the United States, they have dealt primarily with so-called 'old' terrorists who are amenable to political suasion (e.g., peace processes) and pragmatic accommodations (e.g., providing 'sanctuary' in exchange for forbearance with respect to the host state's territory and assets) as well as 'hard' counter-terrorism measures.[21] Such measures are not appropriate for dealing with al-Qaeda: by its terms, bin Laden's offer of a truce to European countries in April 2004 sought to establish a European sanctuary from which Islamic terrorists could confront the US, the existence of which was the crux of the security deficit that enabled the 11 September attacks. Nevertheless, some European countries (like Belgium) have not faced substantial terrorist threats of any kind, and have neither a long counter-terrorism track record nor a cohesive counter-terrorism plan.[22] Thus, European counter-terrorism résumés are not completely attuned to the current problem.

Europe continues to approach terrorism as primarily a risk-management problem to be handled with a threat-based security system, whereby specific emergent risks are assessed and minimised. In roughly equal parts, this is due to scepticism (born more of experience than ignorance) about the ability of government to eliminate vulnerabilities, a relative lack of resources, institutional incapacity and social policy. For example, in late 2003, following increased intelligence-based warnings of attacks involving civilian airliners over the winter holidays and the cancellation or delay of several Europe-to-US flights, the US stated that it would require armed sky marshals on certain transatlantic flights to American destinations. The reluctance of European jurisdictions to enforce compliance among airlines reflected the difference between European nations that have a counter-terrorism culture of risk management – borne of a wealth of experience with 'old' terrorism, including campaigns of deliberate hoaxes – and the United States' vulnerability-based approach that stresses risk minimisation. Even so, in recognition of the graver threat posed by 'new' mass-casualty terrorism, European governments and airlines have compromised. In December 2003, the European Commission agreed to authorise US electronic access to 34 categories of passenger information, while the US agreed to shorten the required duration of data storage from 50 to three-and-a-half years, to an annual joint review of the data-sharing arrangement, and to EU authorities' right to lodge complaints on behalf of EU citizens.

Washington still preferred a broader definition than Brussels of 'serious crime' for which data could be used by law enforcement, and wanted information in 60 categories instead of just 34.

Moreover, there is no doubt that the awareness among national European authorities that Europe was infiltrated by al-Qaeda energised Europe-wide law-enforcement efforts.[23] But the EU is not a United States of Europe, and simply lacks the supranational power to effect and harmonise simultaneous changes in the policies of its constituent national governments. This deficit has a greater impact on territorial security than on proactive law enforcement narrowly construed. For example, it would be politically difficult for the EU to enact comprehensive regulations on port security, terrorism insurance or first-response capacities, as the United States is doing.

Border security is an especially problematic area. Cross-border terrorist threats to European countries are especially acute in light of Europe's southern exposure to the Middle East and North Africa. For instance, while about 300,000 Moroccans reside legally in Spain, tens of thousands are there illegally. Given the virulence of Moroccan radicalisation revealed by the Madrid bombings and the corresponding need to ease the Spanish authorities' domestic monitoring burdens, securer borders constitute an obvious European priority. The Schengen arrangements mandate strict border controls between new EU member states and non-member states. At the same time, open continental borders within an expanding union are integral to the EU's post-modern economic and political experiment.[24] As of May 2004, eight EU member states – Belgium, Denmark, Finland, Ireland, Portugal, Spain, Sweden and the UK – had adopted an EU arrest warrant, which came into force on 1 January 2004. It was first used in Spain on 7 January 2004 – in arresting a Swede on drunk-driving and drug charges filed by Swedish authorities. In theory, the weakening of national borders should ease the application of such warrants to an expanded roster of terrorist organisations. But against that ideal, there is potential for significant member-state backlash. As the EU moves with trepidation towards enhancing its political power, European governments are becoming more worried about haemorrhaging national authority. The target date for the EU arrest warrant to become operational has been steadily pushed back. Differing law-enforcement philosophies may cause other countries to drag their feet on executing warrants, even though legal grounds may be lacking. France, for instance, leans towards direct suppression of radical Islamic sentiment, while Britain often prefers to let militants gather and talk freely and gain intelligence from surveillance.[25]

In May 2002, the European Commission announced the possibility of a multinational EU border patrol that would work with Europol. A 15-day trial was held in which guards from EU member states had patrolled the borders of France, Italy and Spain, stopping 4,500 illegal immigrants and arresting 34 alleged drug traffickers. But, although an EU border patrol was approved in principle at the EU Summit in Seville in June 2002, the EU interior ministers' meeting in Luxembourg in the same month resulted in near-paralysis on border security and immigration issues, mainly over financial and refugee burden-sharing concerns. An EU-wide border patrol is not contemplated as being operational until 2007. Meanwhile, the counter-terrorism potential of those immigration-control devices that have been implemented has been seriously diluted by civil-liberties concerns. On 14 January 2003, the European Automated Fingerprints Identification System – known as 'Eurodac' – was launched in 14 EU member-states plus Norway and Iceland. Designed to monitor and curtail 'asylum shopping', the system registers in a central and commonly accessible database in Brussels the fingerprints of asylum applicants over the age of 14 and certain other illegal immigrants. The system, based on American technology, has impressive technical capabilities: it can run up to 500,000 fingerprint comparisons per second, with better than 99.9% precision.[26] The European Commission required that no information acquired or developed by Eurodac under the supervision of immigration authorities be provided to police or intelligence services.[27] Since the Madrid bombings, however, the Commission has recognised the need to enhance access to information by law-enforcement agencies throughout Europe.

The Schengen Information System (SIS) – in which 13 EU members plus Norway and Iceland participate – is potentially a useful tool. Each participant is required to issue alerts on illegal aliens from outside the EU seeking visas, including authorised documentary, photographic and biometric means of identification. Eurodac is an element of the system. While the EU has allocated funding for extending the SIS to new members, which are required to apply the system, the existing restrictions on access to Eurodac and a general reluctance to impose additional biometric requirements circumscribes the security utility of the SIS. In fact, visa overstays remain a serious EU problem. In countries that are traditionally liberal with respect to immigration, tighter asylum laws have met with considerable public and indeed official outcry. In the UK, for example, proposed legislation curtailing asylum-seekers' right of appeal, cutting legal aid, withdrawing state economic support from rejected families that refuse to leave the country, stiffer penalties for destroying travel documents and cracking down on unscrupulous or unqualified immigration advisers faced parliamentary resistance in early 2004.

Broadly speaking, territorial security in Europe in the near-term is likely to redound mainly to national governments that have customarily handled terrorist threats rather than multilateral organisations.[28] Even after Madrid, it may take an increase in Islamist terrorist attacks on European soil to inspire greater transnational efforts. In the meantime, it will be difficult for national authorities to keep real-time tabs on the influx and outflow of foreigners and Europe will probably remain vulnerable to terrorist infiltration. Persistently lower threat perceptions elsewhere in Europe are likely to dictate more circumspect approaches, especially with respect to intrusions on privacy and civil liberties. There are, for example, considerable barriers to achieving European public-private cooperation at levels comparable to those now being approached in the US.[29] US programmes like C-TPAT require that private company employees submit to government security background checks, and the CSI would plainly benefit from such safeguards. But some European businesses, notably those in Germany, have resisted government intrusions on the privacy of their employees, even when they are premised on counter-terrorism.[30] The EU, with the support of many European telecommunications companies, resisted an American request to increase the period under the EU Directive on Data Protection for Digital Communications during which companies must retain data to permit law-enforcement agencies to comb log files in counter-terrorism investigations, finally accepting retention for only a 'limited period'.[31]

Given the political constraints on building supranational power in the EU, Europe may not collectively develop the community competence required to impose territorial security as repletely as the US. While, for instance, the US regards Europe's data-protection standards as a serious limitation on counter-terrorism cooperation, an umbrella agreement whereby the EU would accept US data privacy standards as adequate for routine transatlantic exchanges may not be possible.[32] But there are some areas in which there is room for a substantial EU contribution. These include passport and visa monitoring, passenger information and container security. In October 2003, ministers from France, Germany, the UK, Italy and Spain met in La Baule, France, to discuss expediting more effective means of addressing immigration and terrorism challenges. French Interior Minister Nicolas Sarkozy proposed the creation of a 'European security zone' to insulate Europe against illegal immigration via the Mediterranean Sea, to be patrolled by North African as well as EU states bordering the sea. The ministers agreed that all common carriers should be required to release passenger data, and mooted the possibility of requiring biometric data in Schengen visas. The Madrid atrocity should allow this higher level of momentum to endure.

Interpol, based in Lyon, France, has established a database of 1.7m stolen passports. It has also devised a system whereby national authorities with access to the database could determine whether individuals were travelling on stolen passports. A 'hit' would lead to bilateral intelligence exchanges between the screening authority and the government from which the suspect passport was stolen. By thus confining the exchange of substantive information only to persons travelling on stolen passports, privacy standards could be upheld. Interpol is also developing analogous systems for checking fingerprints and DNA samples, and in August 2004 urged more governments to join its information network.[33]

Prospects for transatlantic convergence
At the heart of the transatlantic debate about security against terrorism is whether preventive and precautionary measures should be adopted more on the basis of vulnerability in light of the potential capabilities of terrorist networks, or on threat-driven analyses of terrorist objectives and modus operandi. Although its approach can be broadly characterised as intelligence-driven, the UK in particular has tried to wed the two modalities in the MI5 assessment process through the Joint Terrorism Analysis Centre (JTAC) at cabinet level. The process involves weighing a subjective assessment of the likelihood that a terrorist will employ a given method with the

damage that will result if it is used. In accordance with that determination, JTAC determines the appropriate allocation of effort to reducing the threat and reducing vulnerability with an eye towards reducing the overall risk.

There have been clear indications of convergence regarding the risks of WMD terrorism. Al-Qaeda's apocalyptic designs bespeak a movement that not only would have no compunction about using WMD, but would consider them ideal strategic tools. This has been the operative assumption of a US government understandably inclined, in the wake of 11 September, to base security policy on the worst case. Nevertheless, the prevailing view in US intelligence circles is that while al-Qaeda and its affiliates would like to develop and use WMD and have tried to gather chemical, biological and nuclear materials, it does not thus far appear to have the capacity to perpetrate WMD attacks. The consistent use of conventional terrorist weapons such as car-bombs or, less often, standard military weapons like surface-to-air missiles, bears out this assessment. Thus, the CIA's unclassified May 2003 threat assessment talks tentatively about the group's 'crude procedures' for making chemical toxins and 'interest in' producing them, while the FBI's National Infrastructure Protection Center bulletin notes that al-Qaeda may have 'experimented with' such procedures.[34] There also appears to be a loose consensus that Islamic terrorists could probably develop WMD capability only with the help of a state or state-affiliated scientists – whether by direct supply, technical assistance or the provision of a permissive operating environment. The US government is coming around to the view that al-Qaeda never established any serious operational links with any state except Sudan prior to 1996 and subsequently Afghanistan under the Taliban, and that these connections did not add appreciably to any inchoate WMD capability on al-Qaeda's part.[35] But revelations that Abdul Qadeer Khan, the father of Pakistan's nuclear bomb, furnished materiel and technical assistance to North Korea, Iran and Libya, have reinforced concerns that rogue scientists could help al-Qaeda advance a WMD capability.[36]

In any case, it is probable that a terrorist group could produce a non-fissionable atomic bomb – also known as a radiological dispersal device or 'dirty bomb' – without state help. Dirty bombs are often labelled weapons of mass 'disruption' as opposed to 'destruction' because they would cause relatively few immediate casualties but still render a commercially critical area of a city off-limits and produce widespread panic over acute and persistent fears of longer-term health effects on the general population. Bin Laden is believed to have expressed a special interest in building a dirty bomb to a former Pakistani nuclear scientist with radical Islamist beliefs in August 2001, but the crudeness and infeasibility of the plans for such a device developed by American al-Qaeda operative José Padilla suggested that the group had no credible capability.

National Security Presidential Directive 17 (NSPD-17) establishes three pillars for US policy for countering WMD threats: counter-proliferation; strengthened non-proliferation; and consequence management.[37] Major US non-proliferation initiatives were of course in place well before 11 September. The Cooperative Threat Reduction (CTR) programme for securing and disposing of fissile material and WMD in Russia and former Soviet territories and finding alternative employment for weapons scientists, which began in the early 1990s, is particularly well suited to preventing WMD from falling into the hands of non-state actors. Federal support for CTR increased after 11 September, and the model may be extended to India and Pakistan. The recognised gap between al-Qaeda's intentions and capabilities has prompted additional forward US measures. Under the CSI, US customs officials are permitted to check container cargo in foreign ports; under the Proliferation Security Initiative, an increasingly large group of countries cooperate in the air, ground and maritime interdiction of vessels suspected of illicitly transporting WMD or related materials. On one hand, the fact that Washington took the lead on both programmes suggests that it perceives a more serious WMD terrorist threat than European capitals. On the other hand, as both initiatives enjoy wide European participation, transatlantic threat perceptions appear to be converging.[38] The EU has also increased its financial commitment to the CTR. As it has become clearer that al-Qaeda and Baghdad had no planning-level connections and Iraq probably had no ready WMD, the Bush administration adopted a more diplomatic and less dire approach to counter-proliferation with respect to North Korea and Iran. On this political level as well, American and European approaches to WMD problems have become more compatible.[39] Libya's recent renunciation of WMD should reinforce rather than hinder this convergence.

Overall, the European conception of security will probably remain more threat-based than the one that the US hopes to effectuate. Moreover, the EU – particularly its new expanded incarnation – does not and will not in the near future possess the supranational power to coordinate the law-enforcement authorities of member states to the extent that the federal government can supervise national, state and local authorities in the US. Nevertheless, transatlantic homeland-security dynamics furnish each European country with a strong incentive to improve its own security via intra-European cooperation, and hybrid approaches like the UK's – which give due weight to vulnerability considerations – reflect potential for conceptual harmonisation. The UK in particular shares American hypersensitivity to threats of weapons of mass destruction or disruption. It has mobilised the military to guard against risks from surface-to-air missiles. Like the US, the UK emphasises civil defence and national resilience, having simulated a chemical attack in central London in September 2003 to sharpen its preparedness. After the Madrid bombings, British authorities reiterated that a major terrorist attack in the UK was 'inevitable'.[40] They are probably as ready to deal with such an attack as any jurisdiction in Europe, having stressed and bolstered civil defence and national resiliency since 11 September.[41] That said, the spectre of an attack on rail systems raises special vulnerability problems. For instance, the UK's 17,000-kilometre, 2,500-station rail network, is used by 5m people a day. Metal detectors and baggage scanners are used only on the Eurostar service running between London and Brussels and London and Paris. Universal airport-style security checks would be impractical and forbiddingly expensive. Security for land-based transportation in the US before the Madrid attacks did not appear to be markedly better than Europe's. The DHS responded with common-sense threat-response and passenger awareness measures and, in May 2004, launched a 30-day pilot railway explosives screening programme.

In many ways, the devil is in the temporal details. Between US and UK security services, it makes a difference whether the issue under discussion involves current threats or those that are extrapolated, say, five years out. If the threat of a massive biological attack were current, both governments would move immediately towards comprehensive preparation, including inoculations and first-response as well as interdiction. The UK, however, is more inclined to conclude that if a significant terrorist capability is likely to materialise in the long term but not presently, health-care spending should not be distorted now to field every possible line of attack. The likelihood that no jurisdiction – including the US – has yet developed the metrics to make a fully informed determination on such questions means that the debate will remain fluid. Longstanding bilateral law-enforcement connections between European countries, and to a lesser extent, the EU's and NATO's existing structures and forums can potentially enhance cooperation within Europe.

Especially after Madrid, American and European substantive counter-terrorism concerns are more likely to converge than diverge. There are considerable complementarities to exploit. The technical capabilities, manpower, reach and resources of US intelligence and its research-and-development capacity are superior, and intelligence provided by the US enhances European governments' capacity to protect their citizens. American warnings about possible terrorist operations in Bali, for example, gave the UK government a basis for alerting British travellers (even if it did not act on it). Further, in the US, public-private cooperation on matters such as border security and cyber-security harnesses the government's security priorities and private companies' incentive to expedite commerce. The US government is discovering that furnishing incentives and 'best practice' guidelines to private industry cannot ensure adequate security for some elements of critical infrastructure, such as chemical and nuclear plants. Nevertheless, European countries could make significant strides in territorial security by effecting public-private partnerships comparable to C-TPAT.

Conversely, Europe has more experience than the US in fighting 'old' terrorist groups, and may have a few things to teach the US about counter-terrorism. Al-Qaeda's growing disposition to engage local actors as contractors, thus blurring the operational distinction between international and domestic terrorism, only raises scope for a European contribution, and for transatlantic cooperation. A profound lack of inter-agency coordination has prompted wholesale soul-searching in existing US law-enforcement and intelligence services and the creation of the DHS. MI5's experience with Northern Irish and other terrorists in the UK may offer American agencies lessons on domestic intelligence collection and coordination and cooperation among civilian, police and military intelligence agencies.

Indeed, the UK's JTAC as well as the United States' Terrorist Threat Integration Center (TTIC), both established since 11 September, have joined up security agencies already and produced more refined operational-level assessments to aid day-to-day tactical action as well as strategic-level assessments to guide policymaking. France has a comparably collegial approach, centred in the Secrétariat Général de la Défense Nationale and spanning the executive and judicial branches of government.

Less traction elsewhere

Owing to institutional weakness or domestic political constraints in jurisdictions outside Europe and North America, gaining traction elsewhere will be more difficult. The challenges to territorial security in Europe – multiple jurisdictions with competing security philosophies and priorities, substantial Muslim populations and porous borders – are amplified in the Asian context. Several other factors come into play. These include: the probable presence of Osama bin Laden and several of his lieutenants in the 'tribal areas' of western Pakistan; the continuing conflict in Kashmir as an inspiration for and source of jihadists; the continued rise of radical Islam and conduct of terrorist training camps in Pakistan; and the constraints imposed on the weak government of Indonesia – which contains the world's largest Muslim population and is prime host to Jemaah Islamiah (Islamic Assembly), a close al-Qaeda affiliate – by radical Islam.

Long before 11 September, al-Qaeda had infiltrated Southeast Asia. In the late 1980s, Osama bin Laden tasked his brother-in-law, Muhammad Jamal Khalifa, to establish himself in the Philippines to funnel money and arms to the Moro Islamic Liberation Front (MILF) and Abu Sayyaf, which sent a substantial number of recruits to Afghanistan for training. Bin Laden also set up a separate al-Qaeda cell in Manila manned by Arabs and headed by Ramzi Yousef and Khalid Shaikh Mohammed, who organised the 1993 World Trade Center bombing. The Manila cell planned to blow up 11 US airliners over the Pacific. In 1995, after the plot went wrong, Yousef fled to Malaysia. He was soon caught in Pakistan and is serving a life sentence in the US, but Khalid Shaikh Mohammed was not apprehended until March 2003 (also in Pakistan) and is believed to have been the key planner of the 11 September operation and to have directed al-Qaeda operations from Karachi. To replace Yousef, bin Laden dispatched Omar al-Faruq to rally Philippine Islamic radicals to attack American interests. Although Abu Sayyaf degenerated into a band of mercenary kidnappers, the MILF opened up four of its own jihadist training camps. After the Philippine government wiped out the main training camp in 2000 and engaged the MILF in peace talks, bin Laden sent Faruq to Indonesia, where he linked up with Jemaah Islamiah. That outfit had begun sending scores of men to al-Qaeda camps in Afghanistan in the early 1990s, and al-Qaeda set up a camp in Sulawesi in 1999. Al-Qaeda has also trained over 100 members of Uighur Muslim separatist groups in China's Xinjiang province, though they appear to present mainly a local threat.

Because of the Association of South-East Asian Nations (ASEAN)'s traditional adherence to the principle of non-interference, the institutional basis for inter-governmental cooperation in the region on security matters is tenuous. While Singapore and Malaysia have been robust counter-terrorism partners, Indonesia's extensive and varied geography, the weakening of Jakarta's control over its provincially based security forces since Suharto's downfall in 1998, and deficiencies in the surveillance and computer capabilities of national authorities required to monitor movements into and out of the country, make border security difficult to achieve despite technical assistance from the US and the EU. Thailand has also appeared less than fully alert to Islamic terrorist threats emanating from its Muslim-dominated southern provinces and from Malaysia. But an upsurge in terrorist violence in early 2004 – coupled with US pressure – appeared to awaken Bangkok to transnational Islamic threats.

Broader pressure from the US and Australia in the wake of terrorist attacks in Indonesia has also enhanced bilateral relationships and produced nascent multilateral counter-terrorism cooperation. In February 2004, at the Bali Regional Ministerial Meeting on Counter-Terrorism, organised jointly by Australia and Indonesia to discuss improving intelligence and investigative cooperation, the two convening countries announced the impending establishment of the Jakarta Centre for Law Enforcement Cooperation (JCLEC). Expected to be operational by the end of 2004, JCLEC will be headed by a senior Indonesian police officer and largely funded by Australia. It will possess both regional capacity-building and operational mandates. The new centre's remit 'to provide operational support and professional guidance in response to specific terrorist threats or actual attacks' distinguished it from the existing US-financed Southeast Asian Regional Centre for Counter-Terrorism in Kuala Lumpur and the International Law Enforcement Academy in Bangkok, which were both restricted to training and research activities. More broadly, a consensus has emerged that maritime security – especially safeguarding oil transport lanes in the Malacca Strait – against terrorist attack is a singularly urgent regional security priority, as their vulnerability has been highlighted by the growing frequency of piracy. While prospects for intensive multilateral cooperation are therefore brightest with respect to maritime security, the missing component remains Indonesia. Between the late 1990s, when piracy began to surge due substantially to instability in Indonesia, and mid-2004, virtually all incidents of piracy occurred in Indonesian waters. Despite evidence that the Indonesian navy and marine police were trying harder, their material resources and the central government's determination to act remain inadequate.

Political Islam in sub-Saharan Africa is neither as prevalent nor as virulent as that in the Gulf, South Asia or Southeast Asia, and the religious makeup of most sub-Saharan African states is more mixed. They are generally not as vulnerable to being hijacked by terrorists as Afghanistan was in the 1990s. Even Somalia, which is homogeneously Sunni Muslim and a chronic failed state, has had only moderate involvement in transnational Islamic terrorism.[42] Nevertheless, terrorist-friendly conditions abound in sub-Saharan Africa.

State weakness is a nearly ubiquitous source of vulnerability there. Weak states (e.g., Congo) interpose a corruptible government apparatus between foreign terrorists and intrusive major powers or treacherous criminal elements, and are therefore more attractive hosts than collapsed or failed states like Somalia.[43] The mercenary and semi-criminal character of some African regimes makes them susceptible to extra-legal influences. Moreover, the state counter-terrorism apparatuses in most African states tend to be under-funded and undermanned, and therefore far less capable than their counterparts in the US, Europe and Asia. Porous borders and the added pressure of heavy refugee flows on overstretched border authorities makes sub-saharan African states easy marks for terrorist infiltrations. These conditions make Western visitors to such states especially attractive targets, as the attack on Israeli tourists in Kenya in November 2002 indicated. Further, in 2003, militants of the Salafist Group for Call and Combat kidnapped 32 European tourists in Algeria and fled from Algerian commandos with 17 of the hostages into Mali before releasing them. Although Mali is the most supportive Muslim country in Africa towards the counter-terrorism campaign, it is also among the poorest and has been unable to develop the capabilities required to cover vast stretches of desert with appropriately trained and armed personnel.

As the Taliban regime in Afghanistan collapsed in late 2001 and the leaders and hard-core fighters of al-Qaeda who were based there dispersed, speculation grew that they would seek refuge in weak African states. Calls arose from the UN, the EU, NGOs and some quarters of the US government for the West to pay greater economic and diplomatic attention to sub-Saharan Africa.[44] In the event, US counter-terrorism agencies concluded that the threat of al-Qaeda reconstituting there was less likely than originally thought, and settled on a preventive approach involving maritime surveillance and interdiction in the Arabian Sea, air surveillance of East Africa from bases in Kenya and a contingent of US Special Forces deployed in Djibouti for reconnaissance quick-reaction and deterrent purposes.

The Kenya attack focused minds in Washington and elsewhere. The region presents a stiff and conceptually basic counter-terrorism challenge for the West: that of nurturing stronger counter-terrorism institutions and, ultimately, states that are less susceptible to terrorist co-optation, while – in the meantime – denying terrorists access to weak African states through military prevention and deterrence.

Due to their proximity to the Persian Gulf and the presence of radical Islamist elements, East Africa and the Horn have constituted the main focus of counter-terrorism concern in sub-Saharan Africa. There is al-Qaeda infrastructure in Kenya and Tanzania dating back to the 1998 US embassy bombings, and the Kenyan assets were utilised in the December 2002 attacks on Israeli targets in Mombasa. The weapons used in these operations came mainly from Somalia, where effective central government is lacking and arms of many varieties circulate freely and can be easily purchased. Somalia, which is also almost entirely Sunni Muslim, was a bolthole for suspects in the December 2002 attacks, and has been the site of al-Qaeda-connected training camps. Although the camps were destroyed in the late 1990s, the fundamentalist organisation al-Ittihaad al-Islamiah is gaining Somali members. While the Ethiopian government vigorously opposes radical Islam, and moderates predominate among Ethiopia's Muslim population, there is an increasingly violent radical fundamentalist minority. The Sudanese government, though not ideologically provocative since 11 September, remains decidedly Islamist. Conversions to Islam in Rwanda – in part a consequence of a loss of Christian faith due to the genocide and the complicity of some priests in the killing – are also on the rise. In addition to establishing the preventive and deterrent counter-terrorism posture in east Africa and the Horn, the US and its partners have extended $100m each in training and financial support to cooperative governments in East Africa and the Horn (under the East Africa Counterterrorism Initiative) and predominantly Muslim Chad, Mali, Mauritania and Niger in north-central Africa (under the Pan-Sahel Initiative). Elsewhere, there are less obvious but still considerable challenges.

Although Kenya and Tanzania are generally viewed as the sub-Saharan African countries most heavily infiltrated by Islamist terrorists, South Africa, home to about 900,000 mainly and ethnically South Asian Muslims, has emerged as a potentially significant recruiting, planning and staging area for al-Qaeda and affiliated operations. In May 2004, the South African national police reported that a terrorist support cell in South Africa had been uncovered earlier in the year. Five operatives were apparently engaged in gathering fake South African passports, and were arrested and deported. Subsequently, a raid on a London safe house yielded a large number of the passports. In July 2004, two Pretoria-based men, Feroz Ganchi and Zubair Ismail, were among 14 terrorist suspects arrested in Gujrat, Pakistan. Pakistani authorities reported that in that raid they recovered documents and maps indicating possible plans to attack the Johannesburg Stock Exchange, the Sheraton Hotel and the US Embassy in Pretoria, the national parliament, a tourist complex in Cape Town and the Queen Elizabeth II cruise-liner in the Durban or Cape Town harbours. Such targeting is broadly consistent with past al-Qaeda-connected operations and planning in, respectively, New York, Jakarta, East Africa, Washington, Bali and the Gulf and the Mediterranean.

Most South African Muslims espouse a moderate and non-confrontational form of Islam, but, as in Indonesia, extremism appears to have gained momentum from the global movement spearheaded by al-Qaeda. Radical Islam has at least three institutional toeholds in South Africa. Two are illegal and have been weakened through law-enforcement efforts. They are the Iran-inspired Qibla (taking its name from the direction towards which Muslims turn to pray, with cells in the Western Cape region); and the perhaps ironically-named People Against Gangsterism and Terrorism (Cape Town-based and included on the US State Department's list of proscribed terrorist organisations in 2001). The Islamic Propagation Center International, whose late founder was virulently anti-Semitic and supportive of Osama bin Laden, is legal and based in Durban, and has been financed by bin Laden's family.

The South African government appears uncertain about whether to characterise the potential indigenous Islamist terrorist problem as serious or marginal. The consensus among outside analysts is that although at odds with certain US policies seen as antagonistic to al-Qaeda (e.g., on the Israeli–Palestinian conflict and Iraq), South Africa's Western values, its commercial and political centrality in sub-Saharan African affairs and its status as an 'anchor state' in major-power geopolitical calculations makes its government at least a tertiary target for Islamist terrorists. More importantly from an operational point of view, several other factors make South Africa an attractive operating environment for support activities. These include: the United States' relative inattention to sub-Saharan Africa; South Africa's sizable Muslim recruitment base; the corruptibility of South African officials; the country's relative commercial sophistication and freedom; its porous borders and proximity to weak states in which weapons flow freely (e.g., Angola and Mozambique); and the presence of mainly Nigerian organised crime networks.

Although the degree of direct Islamist terrorist involvement of West Africa may have fallen short of post-11 September Western expectations, general political instability and the continued viability of Islamist enclaves in countries such as Nigeria, Côte d'Ivoire and Senegal render the region presumptively vulnerable to infiltration. Al-Qaeda or its affiliates appear to have become involved in the illicit West African trade in diamonds and other commodities in the late 1990s, and to have responded to increased surveillance of conventional financial facilities by moving more assets into that trade with the help of now-deposed Liberian President Charles Taylor – though hard evidence is scant. (Evidence of Hizbullah's involvement is more substantial.)

Nigeria's potential strategic importance to the global jihadist movement has been under-appreciated. Nigeria has the largest overall population (about 130m) in sub-Saharan Africa, its largest Muslim population (roughly 65m) and the eighth largest worldwide. While inter-religious tensions have not threatened outright civil war, Christian/Muslim violence has produced thousands of fatalities since 1999, most recently, in 2004, in the central state of Plateau. Further, Western oil interests furnish targets of relatively high political and economic value (on which jihadists have increasingly focused in Iraq and Saudi Arabia). More generally, bin Laden's vision of global jihad resonates at the grassroots level in Nigeria. In January 2002, the BBC reported that seven out of ten male children born at a hospital in the town of Kano in predominantly Muslim northern Nigeria were being given the name 'Osama'. In 2004, inter-communal riots occurred when Muslims became convinced that polio vaccines were part of a Western plot to sterilise Muslims. Sharia law has been introduced into 12 Nigerian states. These factors suggest that Nigeria could become a major recruiting node for al-Qaeda.

While the United States has been strategically preoccupied by problems in Iraq and elsewhere, oil and the potential for terrorist support to thrive in the region have sustained its close attention and will likely continue to do so. Oil interests in Angola, Cameroon, Equatorial Guinea, Gabon and Sao Tome & Principe as well as Nigeria – increasingly important to long-term US hopes of diversifying oil supplies and depending less on the Middle East – are accessible from the Gulf of Guinea and therefore vulnerable. A Congressionally-commissioned study by the Center for Strategic and International Studies in 2004 advised the US government to increase intelligence and counter-terrorism efforts in Africa, to increase financial support for training and equipping African security forces from $10m to $100m, and to devote another $100m to African peace initiatives under the State Department's African Contingency Operations Training and Assistance (ACOTA) programme, for which only $15m was requested for FY2005. Such an expansion of aid would augment existing American support for counter-terrorism efforts in East Africa and north-central Africa. US officials have also contemplated funding a deep-water port – and potentially a US military base – on Sao Tome & Principe and deploying naval assets to monitor the Gulf of Guinea for terrorist threats. European countries – especially France and the UK – too have oil interests as well as residual colonial obligations that tend to sustain their concern for stability and security in West Africa.

Global security?

Whatever the obstacles North America and Europe may face in securing their territory against transnational terrorist threats, those confronted by other regions are considerably greater. In the short term, homeland security as a counter-terrorism instrument of denial may amount to a mere aspiration in countries outside North America and Europe. In the longer term, American and European political and economic pressure on and assistance to foreign governments – motivated by the need to protect trade and citizens overseas – and the prospect that stronger homeland protection in the US and Europe will eventually shift al-Qaeda's operational focus to other regions are likely to yield some homeland-security improvements in those regions. Meanwhile, containing terrorism in such locales will not depend primarily on indigenous homeland-security measures.

In areas where law-enforcement and intelligence institutions are weak or compromised and terrorists are physically concentrated or hold territory – e.g., the Philippines and potentially Somalia – military forces may have a relatively strong default counter-terrorism role. To the extent that those forces are not up to the counter-terrorism challenge, as appears to be the case in the Philippines, the security problem is compounded. One option is for major powers to lend direct outside assistance, but this is limited by domestic political circumstances. In the Philippines, a US special-operations deployment of fewer than 1,000 troops – mainly as advisers, with circumscribed rules of engagement – was politically controversial. Political circumstances in Indonesia and Malaysia effectively bar any foreign combat troops from being deployed. In a similar vein, US soldiers stationed in eastern Afghanistan are inhibited in conducting operations over the Pakistani border, where bin Laden and other al-Qaeda holdouts are believed to be hiding, due to the domestic anti-Western opinion that Pakistani President

Musharraf must accommodate. Likewise, as of August 2004, Malaysia and Indonesia remained wary of US navy patrols in the Malacca Strait as an effective infringement of their sovereignty.

In the medium term, the way around this on the operational level is for the US and other developed nations to fund counter-terrorism training for civilian and military institutions in, and share intelligence and technical surveillance capacity with, counter-terrorism 'partners of concern'. In sub-Saharan Africa, the Pan Sahel Initiative is a good start. Meanwhile, the key ingredients of territorial security in such places will be the efforts of the US and other major powers to deny transnational terrorists' access to those places, coupled with their proactive law-enforcement and intelligence cooperation with regional governments.

Chapter 2

Law-enforcement and Intelligence Capabilities

The increased saliency of terrorism in Southeast Asia signalled by the 13 October 2002 bombing of the Sari Club and Paddy's Bar in Bali, which was planned in Thailand, refocused broader international efforts to combat terrorism proactively. As well as a large number of Indonesians, the 202 victims included 88 Australians, Europeans from several countries and Americans. Significantly, the Bali bomb intentionally targeted Christian tourists from Western cultures without regard to specific nationality or the fate of native Balinese (most of whom are non-Muslim). According to Imam Samudra, a confessed planner of the operation arrested by Indonesian police in November 2002, the targets were chosen simply because 'a lot of foreigners' frequented them.[1] Five days before the Bali bombing, al-Qaeda-linked terrorists in Kuwait strafed US Marines who were training there with assault rifles, killing one. These attacks illuminated al-Qaeda's increasingly flexible targeting strategy – embracing all Jews, Christians and potentially Hindus as well as distinctly American assets – and drove home the point that comprehensive counter-terrorism requires of European, Asian and Middle Eastern countries as well as the United States forward intelligence and law-enforcement capabilities.

The Madrid bombings on 11 March 2004 – which killed 191 and was perpetrated by North African Islamists affiliated with al-Qaeda – constituted another watershed. Before Madrid, it appeared that the US and European counter-terrorism measures had been provisionally able to deny al-Qaeda and its affiliates access to Western territory and opportunities to commit terrorist acts on

Western ground and, post-Afghanistan, had forced the organisation to focus on soft targets of opportunity in countries with weak or otherwise compromised counter-terrorism institutions. But the Iraq intervention reinforced bin Laden's claims that the West seeks to dominate and exploit Islam and revivified his primal grievance – US occupation of sacred Arab Muslim land. Thus, Iraq intensified the terrorist urge to strike the West and increased the global movement's recruiting power, partially offsetting improvements in cooperation among counter-terrorism partners.

With the Madrid attacks and arguably those in Istanbul in November 2003, al-Qaeda and its affiliates appeared to move away from their immediate post-11 September soft-targeting dispensation to more sharply anti-Western operations of greater political value. Escalating up the chain of American allies from tentative to strong – Saudi Arabia, Turkey and then Spain – transnational Islamist terrorists seemed fully reconstituted in a flatter and more atomised arrangement, back on the offensive and focusing on Western targets. US agencies did develop intelligence suggesting that certain functions – in particular, bomb manufacture – may be more centralised and therefore potentially more efficient and sophisticated than earlier believed.[2] On balance, however, al-Qaeda remained an even more horizontal and less hierarchical organisation than it had been before the Afghanistan intervention. The connections between al-Qaeda's hardcore leadership and its local assets appear to have become essentially ideological and inspirational rather than operational. That leadership continues to provide vision and direction for the global movement, but must rely increasingly on local affiliates or sympathizers to prosecute its violent agenda. Still, there remain significant operational liaisons – such as Abu Musab al-Zarqawi, the Jordanian operating in Iraq apparently for both al-Qaeda and Ansar al-Islam – between al-Qaeda and local groups. Investigations of post-11 September terrorist operations also indicate that local groups are led by or enlist individuals who have been to al-Qaeda training camps for ideological indoctrination and operational training. So fairly durable substantive links to the father institution, as it were, have survived.

Transatlantic divergences and convergences
Broadly construed, Europe may be al-Qaeda's highest-value 'field of jihad' other than the United States. Benjamin and Simon note that

Europe's substantial number of youthful socially and politically marginalised Muslims 'has been mobilized by al-Qaeda for the assault against the Crusaders on their own territory. From the shores of Europe, they will reach the heart of the far enemy. That, anyway, is the plan'.[3] Bin Laden's audiotape warning to France, Germany, Italy and the UK that any assistance construed as anti-Muslim that they extended to the US would meet with al-Qaeda reprisals intimated that al-Qaeda still saw Europe as a potential redoubt as well as a prime target. By implication, the same goes for his post-Madrid 'reconciliation initiative' to stop terrorist operations against any European country whose government 'commits itself to not attacking Muslims or interfering with their affairs'. Consequently, pursuing and apprehending terrorists in Europe is key to the overall goal of neutralising al-Qaeda. This places premiums both on European intelligence and law-enforcement capabilities that are robust in their own right and on transatlantic counter-terrorism cooperation.[4]

Europe's experience with terrorism

Europe has more experience with terrorism than does the United States. Starting in the 1960s, the United Kingdom faced threats from the Provisional IRA, which sought to unite Ireland by force, as well as Irish republican splinter groups and pro-state 'loyalist' paramilitaries drawn from Northern Ireland's Protestant working-class. Spain confronted the Basque separatists of Euskadi ta Askatasuna (ETA), who mounted a terrorist insurgency similar to that of the IRA, with which it developed close links. Germany had to deal with the leftist Baader-Meinhof Gang and Red Army Faction. The Red Brigades waged a brutal Marxist-Leninist campaign against the Italian government, which included the torture and execution of former Prime Minister Aldo Moro in 1978 and as recently as 2002 the assassination of a government economic adviser. Greece was afflicted (and its law-enforcement and intelligence agencies probably infiltrated) by the ultra-nationalist, anti-American Revolutionary Organisation 17 November for over 25 years, and a new anti-Western group called Revolutionary Struggle claimed responsibility for bombings on a judicial complex in September 2003 and a police station in May 2004.

Against these groups, the criminalisation of terrorism, the aggressive use of informants and infiltrators, and the institutionalisation of public vigilance (e.g., abandoned luggage alerts) and security checks (e.g., bag searches at commercial establishments) fleshed out European national counter-terrorism programmes. Furthermore, most of the European terrorist groups used violence with restraint to preserve a place at the negotiating table, or at least to constrain adversaries' direct provocations, and to an extent could be politically tamed. Some political measures were more effective than others. Conflict resolution in Northern Ireland, culminating in the Good Friday Agreement of 1998, quieted the IRA. But the French 'sanctuary doctrine', whereby terrorist support activity in France was tolerated provided terrorist operations were not directed at French interests, ultimately failed to placate the Algeria-based Armed Islamic Group (GIA), which carried out nine attacks on French soil in the mid-1990s.

In 1995, French authorities moved decisively from any remnant of the capitulatory sanctuary doctrine (narrowed to that of 'accommodation' in the 1980s) to prevention, and expeditiously rolled up the GIA cells responsible for the recent attacks.[5] Even before that, the increasingly violent European activity of 'international' terrorist groups like the Palestine Liberation Organisation (PLO) and the Lebanese anti-Israeli group Hizbullah in the 1970s and 1980s suggested that atomised, government-by-government counter-terrorism measures were insufficient. The TREVI (the French acronym for 'Terrorism, Radicalism, Extremism and International Violence') arrangement among European Community governments, under which they regularly discussed security problems at ministerial level, was inaugurated in 1976. This multinational collaboration produced some highly effective joint operations against international terrorist groups, including the dismantling of Hizbullah's Western European network in 1987.

While rudimentarily networked counter-terrorism capabilities are thus not entirely new to Europe, the 'new terrorist' threat now facing the US and the 'old terrorist' threats that generally afflicted Europe constitute only a limited source of unity. The European activities of the PLO and Hizbullah in the 1970s and 1980s were undertaken mainly to serve local objectives within their respective regions or countries of origin, did not seek to debilitate European governments and did not globally disperse anywhere near the number of operatives that al-Qaeda has done. As noted earlier, al-

Qaeda's transnational threat is different in kind from that posed by the IRA or even Hamas. Al-Qaeda has little interest in overt bargaining. Bin Laden did not really expect any government to be craven enough to expressly take him up on his truce offer in April 2004, and intended mainly to intimidate European capitals into distancing themselves from Washington. Unlike any European terrorist cadre, al-Qaeda's leadership seeks to cripple the US by inflicting mass casualties – potentially with WMD.[6] European officials are, of course, aware of these distinctions. At the same time, European capitals' approach to counter-terrorism is inevitably informed by their respective experiences with essentially old terrorist threats.[7] On balance, then, while European governments that have experienced terrorism retain the operational culture required to maintain a sustained, high-tempo counter-terrorism profile, they have been called upon to orient themselves to a terrorist threat that is unprecedentedly difficult to hedge by political means.

Counter-terrorism in Europe since 11 September

Generally, European governments have not mobilised to the degree that the US has done. Before 11 September, only six EU members – France, Germany, Italy, Portugal, Spain and the UK – had specific counter-terrorism legislation as distinct from ordinary criminal codes. Others, such as The Netherlands, responded to 11 September with specific plans of action or legislative reforms. Some, like Belgium, have not done so.

The statutory counter-terrorism regimes already in place in the six countries to combat old terrorist threats arguably provided them with a structural head start in countering transnational terrorism, and several have been strengthened by new anti-terrorist legislation or increased enforcement efforts.[8] Spanish magistrates, seasoned by the longstanding Basque terrorism problem and equipped with tough counter-terrorism laws, have been among the most dogged pursuers of al-Qaeda suspects. Germany has substantially increased funding for the federal border guard, the federal prosecutor's office and the intelligence agencies, and increased law-enforcement access to personal financial data. It has also authorised the prosecution of foreigners associated with foreign terrorist organisations based outside Germany and the deportation of those perpetrating political violence or otherwise threatening Germany's 'basic order of democratic freedom'. Italy has similarly broadened statutory authority for apprehending terrorists. Yet the enthusiasm of the Spanish judiciary belied a myopic complacency about transnational Islamic terrorism at the law enforcement and intelligence level: before the Madrid bombings, only 80 officers were assigned to cover externally-based terrorist threats; ETA though crippled, was still considered the primary danger.[9] The German and Italian measures could be viewed as largely remedial. Both Germany and Italy were hampered by bureaucratic inefficiencies and significant statutory gaps in their law-enforcement regimes. Prior to 11 September, for instance, Germany had no provision outlawing foreign-based terrorist organisations and Italy did not authorise surveillance of those suspected of membership in such organisations.

While British authorities agree that the US is still al-Qaeda's principal target, they rate the UK prime among its European targets on account of the presence of significant American and Israeli targets in the UK, the insularity and increasing radicalisation of its Muslim population, the UK's political alignment with the US, and the UK's traditional 'special relationship' and historical links with the United States. Well before 11 September, Osama bin Laden was at the top of the threat list of Government Communications Headquarters (GCHQ), the UK's signals intelligence agency, and the UK expanded its list of proscribed terrorist organisations to cover Islamic terrorist groups in February 2001, six months before the 11 September attacks. Accordingly, the UK has been exceptionally urgent in responding to 11 September. In December 2001, the UK parliament passed laws comparable in effect to the USA PATRIOT Act, including requirements that communications companies retain accessible records of calls made and e-mails sent (though not their contents), more rigorous record-keeping requirements for transport companies, enhanced financial surveillance and restriction authorisation, provisions for greater inter-agency exchange of intelligence and a controversial power of indefinite detention applicable to suspected international terrorists. In June 2002, a security and intelligence coordinator at permanent-secretary rank was appointed. Also that June, the government announced plans to form a 6,000-strong reaction force (to be drawn partly from the Territorial Army, the volunteer reserve body) to assist police and civil authorities in the event of a mass-casualty attack in Britain. (By comparison, France's Directorate of Territorial Security has about 1,500 employees.) In November 2002, Parliament passed legislation barring asylum-seekers from working and requiring them to be housed in isolated reception camps. UK Home Secretary David Blunkett has tightened asylum criteria and vested immigration officials with the authority to reject automatically asylum claims of those from countries determined to be safe. Finally, the Metropolitan Police Service's Anti-Terrorism Squad, in conjunction with local police special branches and in cooperation with the FBI, has moved aggressively against UK residents suspected of helping al-Qaeda prepare or recruit for terrorist operations.

At the multinational level, police in each EU member-state have the right of hot pursuit into other EU countries, and in May 2002 France and Germany agreed in principle that each country's law-enforcement authorities could make arrests on the other's soil. France reached a similar arrangement with Belgium. On balance, however, the EU's counter-terrorism effort has been more aspirational than substantive. The creation of ad hoc and temporary joint teams of law-enforcement officers from two or more member states to investigate cross-border crimes had been authorised in October 1999, and their remit was expanded to terrorism after 11 September. The EU Counter-Terrorism Task Force – composed of one police and one intelligence representative from each EU member-state, plus about ten Europol officials for administrative and operational support – was also set up in late September 2001. The unit liaises with US counterparts and collects and analyses information and intelligence on transnational threats, and was charged with drafting a joint terrorist threat assessment. On 21 September 2001, EU leaders decided in an emergency session to enhance EU-wide police and judicial cooperation, plug sources of terrorist financing and enhance EU–US law-enforcement cooperation. They also approved a work programme embracing 30 initiatives on law-enforcement cooperation within the EU and external border controls, including a common EU definition of terrorism, the EU-wide arrest warrant, networked border monitoring and control, a common visa policy among member states and Eurodac.[10]

There is a high degree of law-enforcement cooperation among European governments, founded on shared problems like narcotics trafficking and 'old' terrorist threats. The most important security relationships are bilateral. Further, they tend to centre around police forces as opposed to intelligence agencies and are generally operational rather than analytical. The habit of cooperation and pre-existing bilateral relationships have clearly benefited counter-terrorism efforts since 11 September. Owing to a kind of bureaucratic peer pressure, European law-enforcement agencies since 11 September have become noticeably more inclined to arrest and detain suspects instead of leaving them circulating to facilitate intelligence-gathering via surveillance and penetration. In January 2003, for example, French, British, Italian and Spanish authorities coordinated police swoops resulting in over 50 arrests of mostly North African terrorist suspects.[11] This reflects an appreciation of the greater risks associated with mass-casualty attacks compared with those of deliberately restrained old-style groups like the IRA or ETA. The source of this new bias is not only the US but also France – the European state with the most experience in dealing with Muslim terrorists – which long chided the UK in particular for electing to watch rather than snatch.

Although some bilateral intelligence relationships have developed through NATO, and the end of the Cold War has relaxed national governments' attitudes towards intelligence-sharing, they still guard their foreign intelligence assets – analyses as well as raw information – jealously. Nevertheless, the Maastricht Treaty's third pillar (for immigration and asylum, policing, customs and legal cooperation), which superseded TREVI, mandated the creation of Europol, which became operational in late 1998. Europol's capabilities, however, are circumscribed. Europol itself embraces only police organisations, has no enforcement powers, is limited to providing analytic and coordinative support for national law-enforcement agencies, and is further constrained by the competing interests of Brussels and national governments.[12] The most it can do is ask national governments to initiate joint investigations of endemic large-scale criminal problems, including terrorism.[13] Although Europol's budget doubled after 11 September to €51.66m and rose to €58.8m in 2003, and its 242-strong staff was set to increase to 485 by the end of 2004, Europol's staff will remain small in absolute terms: its counter-terrorism unit was to expand to a mere 20 over five years. The organisation is seeking to consolidate through its offices a fluent multinational network of law-enforcement professionals, and now includes in its headquarters in The Hague liaison officers from each EU country who facilitate interaction between Europol and 34 law-enforcement agencies. In December 2001, Europol also established a formal liaison arrangement with US law-enforcement agencies and opened a liaison office in Washington the following August. Under the new transatlantic relationship, 'strategic' or 'technical' information – threat tips, crime patterns, risk assessments and investigative procedures – can be shared.[13] But the more significant and deep operational and intelligence relationships within Europe are likely to remain bilateral for the foreseeable future.

Transatlantic cooperation
Notably heavy radical Islamic activity in support of terrorism has been uncovered in Germany, the United Kingdom and France, all of which have large Muslim populations.[15] There are about 15m Muslims in Western Europe. This is considerably higher than the American Muslim population. The US Census Bureau is forbidden to inquire about religious affiliation, so estimates of the US Muslim population vary widely. But while they have reached as high as 8m, the fairest estimate appears to be about 3m.[16] Yet European governments cannot afford the counter-terrorism resources that the US can: even the UK's approach is primarily intelligence-driven, designed to respond to threats sequentially, as they arise, so that resources are optimally channelled towards the most immediate priorities. Political factors in Europe bar the kind of integrated approach to counter-terrorism that the United States' single federal jurisdiction permits. Transatlantic cooperation therefore tends to be actuated by separate and vigorously serviced American bilateral engagements with European capitals. The most substantial of these is the relationship between the US and the UK, which was already singularly strong by virtue of their traditional 'special relationship' and further intensified after 11 September. The US and the UK share most intelligence related to counter-terrorism. But bilateral exchanges between Washington and other European capitals were also built up during the Cold War, and have been enhanced since 11 September. More focused post-11 September transatlantic cooperation has produced clear results. Over 500 arrests had been made in European jurisdictions by early 2004, often with the intelligence or operational assistance of a second country, and a couple of dozen of those arrested had been convicted of terrorist offences.

Although Muslims in Europe far outnumber those in the United States, six months after the 11 September attacks the number of related arrests made in the US exceeded arrests in Europe by a factor of roughly five.[17] European authorities have had some success in connecting those arrested to al-Qaeda and convicting them. Their approach has stayed more strictly within the boundaries of traditional law enforcement than does the American approach, which in some respects has hybridised civil law enforcement and the law of armed conflict. Neither approach appears functionally superior to the other. By the same token, Europeans are less comfortable with measures that appear unnecessary and merely expedient taken by states that do have strong enforcement and judicial institutions. One prominent example is the United States' imprisonment of over 600 battlefield detainees at Guantanamo Bay in Cuba and the proposed use of military tribunals to try them, to which European governments have objected.[18]

Virtually all European governments have domestic intelligence agencies empowered to collect as well as analyse information on citizens and residents. The US does not have any such agency and will probably remain devoid of one unless there is another major 11 September-style attack on US territory.[19] But three factors have blunted Europe's edge: (1) EU data-protection standards that are stricter than the United States' standards; (2) the USA PATRIOT Act's statutory erosion of the wall between domestic intelligence and law enforcement by way of increasing the FBI's powers; and (3) the advent of the Terrorist Threat Integration Center (TTIC). In early 2003, the Director of Central Intelligence (DCI) formed TTIC from elements of the DHS, the FBI's Counterterrorism Division, the DCI's Counterterrorism Center and the Department of Defense. With access to the full range of raw and polished intelligence, TTIC is supposed to optimise the use of information on terrorist threats, expertise and capabilities; to analyse intelligence and refine its collection; to enhance the government bureaucracy to ensure robust inter-agency intelligence-sharing; to integrate foreign and domestic intelligence on terrorist threats; and to present those assessments to the national political leadership. TTIC also maintains a database of known and suspected terrorists that will be accessible to federal, state and local authorities.[20]

Transatlantic strategic policy differences and a few episodes of counter-terrorism dyspepsia belie overall day-to-day operational harmony, for which there are strong incentives. The organisational flatness, pragmatism and transnational ubiquity of the al-Qaeda network means that the operational distinction between international and domestic terrorism has become more obscure. Post-Afghanistan, al-Qaeda has had to rely increasingly on more traditional, locally or regionally focused terrorist organisations whose modus operandi more closely resembles that of European terrorist groups.[21] Improvements in US homeland security make America less vulnerable, while the European authorities' post-11 September counter-terrorism re-orientation towards greater vigilance make Europe a more challenging operating environment for terrorists. These factors have rendered Europe a more attractive direct al-Qaeda target than it was before 11 September.[22] Consequently, the United States' global priorities and the European experience with domestic terrorism appear increasingly compatible, and the opportunities for mutual benefit increasingly rich.[23]

Accordingly, policy differences have been finessed. For example: in spite of the transatlantic dispute on the protection of airline-passenger data, satisfactorily resolved only in May 2004, since March 2003 European authorities have informally provided their American counterparts with credit-card details and addresses of US-bound passengers in advance of their arrival. After months of delay, French and German authorities finally agreed in November 2002 to provide the US with the requested information on suspected 'twentieth hijacker' Zacarias Moussaoui on condition that it not be used as evidence in support of a death sentence.[24] Similarly, the EU's counter-terrorism task force and the FBI have exchanged personal data on those suspected of involvement in the 11 September attacks on the basis of a special EU exemption covering 'life-threatening situations'. Data-protection preoccupations, like the continuing denial of Eurodac access to intelligence officials, constitute a more serious problem; a comparable lack of inter-agency transparency contributed to the US security failure on 11 September.

Future transatlantic challenges are likely to turn more on institutional dysfunction than divergent threat perceptions. As its two primary multinational organisations seek to accommodate enlarged memberships, Europe will probably find harmonised and collective action harder to produce. The US, in that case, will increasingly rely on firm, but still ad hoc, bilateral linkages. Such an arrangement cuts against efficiency and institutionalisation, which are preferable in the sustained mobilisation that the 'war' on terror requires.

Softer targets

Clearly the improvements in hard counter-terrorist measures – both homeland security and proactive enforcement – in the United States and Europe forced al-Qaeda and its affiliates opportunistically to seek softer targets in other parts of the world, including Indonesia, Kenya, Kuwait, Morocco, Saudi Arabia, Tunisia, Turkey and of course Iraq. Some of its second-choice targets are nonetheless perceived as strong US counter-terrorism partners. Since 11 September, the Pakistani government has established its bona fides in the campaign against terrorism by extending tactical assistance during *Operation Enduring Freedom*, cooperating with the CIA and the FBI, and arresting (as of February 2003) over 400 al-Qaeda suspects and handing most of them over to US authorities. Among those apprehended and transferred to the US are high-ranking al-Qaeda leaders Khalid Shaikh Mohammed and Abu Zubeida. Pakistani leader Pervez Musharraf's cooperation with the West, however, is still subject to significant constraints. The influence of Islamic radicalism in Pakistan is large and growing; the more Musharraf cracks down on terrorism – both al-Qaeda- and Kashmir-related – the more difficult it is for him to control the radical segment of the population. Furthermore, the 10,000-strong Inter-Services Intelligence directorate (ISI) is heavily Islamised and may be providing limited tactical help to al-Qaeda. This could include passively assisting bin Laden, second-in-command Ayman al-Zawahiri and Taliban leader Mullah Omar by not revealing where they are hiding.

Indonesia presents problems analogous to Pakistan's, but less pronounced. Indonesian President Megawati Sukarnoputri's secularist government has needed to appease the Central Axis grouping of Muslim parties that brought her to power in July 2001. These parties, some of which have close relations with local extremists, share an anti-Western attitude and resentment of US economic, political and military power. Immediately after 11 September, then Vice-President Hamzah Haz, an Islamist and an open admirer of bin Laden, claimed the attacks on Washington and New York would 'cleanse the US of its sins'. Another problem is the scale and intractability of Indonesia's numerous internal security problems in Aceh, Papua, Maluku, Kalimantan and Central Sulawesi, which have sometimes called Indonesia's continuing national cohesion into doubt and deflected the security forces' attention from terrorist threats. Resistance from within Indonesia's factionalised and demoralised security forces has also undermined Jakarta's willingness and ability to cooperate. The armed forces fear confronting Islamic extremists, which could seriously exacerbate domestic tensions in the run-up to the 2004 presidential election. Indeed, the military has cultivated links with certain radical Islamic movements and militias as part of a wider political tactic not only to maintain the armed forces' political influence, but also to balance the perceived danger of a leftist revival while undermining the potential threat from militants intent on establishing an Islamic state.[25]

Indonesian authorities are not hopeless. In fact, their human intelligence is considered excellent, they have undoubtedly penetrated some terrorist networks and State Intelligence Director Abdullah Mahmud Hendropriyono is resolutely secular and hard-line. But their intelligence analysis is traditionally weak, which may indicate the persistence of the influences of political Islam in Indonesian government and a disinclination to admit the worst.[26] Until after the Bali bombing, for example, Jakarta refused to admit that Jemaah Islamiah (JI) constituted a transnational threat despite its having a pan-Islamic objective – a sharia-based caliphate covering Indonesia, Singapore, Brunei, Malaysia and the southern Philippines – that is highly compatible with al-Qaeda's objectives; strong evidence of sympathies and operational connections between Indonesian members of the group and al-Qaeda; the revelation in December 2001 of a JI plot to hit US, British, Israeli and Australian targets in Singapore; and consequent indications that the group had operational capabilities in Singapore, Malaysia and the Philippines as well as Indonesia.[27]

Pressure from outside powers – especially the US, the EU and Australia – have sporadically energised Indonesian law-enforcement efforts. In the immediate aftermath of the Bali bombing the Indonesian authorities apprehended three major suspects, two of whom confessed. Later another dozen suspects were arrested, and Jakarta publicly reversed its position the JI was not a threat. The spiritual leader of the JI network, Abu Bakar Bashir, was arrested

– though initially on immigration charges and only later, in 2004, for terrorism. With help from US and Thai authorities, Indonesian agencies intensified the search for Riduan Isamuddin, the Indonesian cleric also known as Hambali who was a member of al-Qaeda's leadership council (shura) and the liaison between al-Qaeda and JI; he was caught in Thailand in August 2003. But again, ASEAN's longstanding policy of non-interference limits scope for inter-governmental counter-terrorism cooperation. In May 2002, for example, Indonesia joined Malaysia and the Philippines to sign a trilateral Agreement on Information Exchange and Establishment of Communications Procedures covering 23 areas of cooperation against terrorism and other cross-border crime, including joint training, exercises and operations as well as intelligence-sharing. Cambodia and Thailand later acceded to the agreement, and more ASEAN countries are expected to sign up. But in October 2002, when the Bali bombing occurred, the joint committee that monitors and applies the provisions of the agreement still had not been formally convened.

Bilateral cooperative mechanisms hold more promise. Following the Bali bombing the US won permission from Malaysia to open a regional counter-terrorism training centre in Kuala Lumpur in 2003. In a similar vein, the EU dispatched a high-level troika to Indonesia to build on regular contacts at expert level and to identify projects for improving counter-terrorism capacity. The EU also pledged to accelerate aid to Indonesia for border monitoring, and to intensify counter-terrorism contacts with Australia. Australia, in turn, moved quickly to establish a permanent intelligence liaison office in Jakarta and, in a flurry of diplomacy, secured memoranda of agreement from Indonesia, Thailand and the Philippines providing for greater Australian involvement in counter-terrorism operations and investigations in those countries.[28] The most fruitful bilateral relationships have arisen with Southeast Asian countries that have longstanding worries about Islamic extremism. Among Southeast Asian countries, Singapore and the Philippines probably have the highest terrorist threat perceptions.[29] Accordingly, they have been the most cooperative with outside powers.

As in Europe, in Asia the United States' most efficacious counter-terrorism relationships are more likely to be bilateral than multilateral. With respect to Europe, pre-existing bilateral transatlantic relationships make the day-to-day activity of counter-terrorism more a matter of management than diplomacy. But in Asia, the relative primitiveness of bilateral relationships between outside powers and regional states puts a premium on diplomacy for purposes of securing a baseline level of standing cooperation. This may involve economic concessions, enhanced military-to-military contacts or the thickening of liaison relationships between civilian agencies. Looking farther forward, enhanced diplomatic relationships between Western and Southeast Asian governments could become an important mechanism for isolating al-Qaeda from 'franchises' like JI. The al-Qaeda leadership itself sees the US as its prime strategic enemy, and regards Europe both tactically, as a platform for attacking the US directly, and strategically, as an element of the West that must eventually be brought to its knees. Al-Qaeda's Southeast Asian and South Asian affiliates are more concerned with local and regional religious and political objectives. This difference is of little operational significance in the short and medium term: the co-optation of the US and its allies and partners through violence serves both al-Qaeda's global agenda and other organisations' regional ones. Changed political, economic and social circumstances, however, could eventually prompt regional groups to assess al-Qaeda's maximalism as unduly costly in political terms, and they may thus make them more amenable to compromise. Any such change is likely to have the greatest persuasive power if it is perceived as coming from indigenous governments, as opposed to Western countries who would be perceived as imperialistic or otherwise hegemonic. Strong but discreet state-to-state relationships would allow Western governments to influence local governments' policies in the right direction without the need for provocative and alienating military interventions, sanctions or coercive diplomacy.

Terrorist financing

Among many counter-terrorism challenges, that of money-laundering and other forms of terrorist financing summons perhaps the highest level of ongoing, day-to-day inter-governmental cooperation. Terrorism is relatively cheap, but it is not free. It requires money for safe houses, salaries and weapons, and to run and sponsor Islamic schools (madrassas), many of which preach radical forms of Islam. This comes from a broad transnational array of sympathisers and 'fellow travellers'. They may contribute to Hamas, Hizbullah or JI – to take just three examples – as well as al-Qaeda itself. The upshot is that to be effective, financial regulators need to cast a wide net that encompasses the entire international matrix of terrorism supporters, and not just al-Qaeda and its known affiliates.

Since 11 September, in both Europe and the United States, regulators have attempted to do just that. Mainstream banking is now subject to substantial vigilance. Major strides in financial surveillance, however, will now be difficult to make. Terrorist groups have effectively improvised in response to the initial crackdown, and still enjoy material support from a large number of individuals and the acquiescence or cooperation of some government officials.

Mainstream banking

Between September 2001 and June 2002, European countries had frozen or seized about $35m in suspected terrorist assets and the US roughly the same amount, out of a total of $115m confiscated worldwide. This has been primarily because banking is heavily regulated in both places, and because the 11 September attacks prompted even stricter oversight of the laundering of money through placement offshore or in charitable fronts, layering funds via multiple transactions and accounts, and integrating illicit monies with legitimate ones. Post-11 September measures include UN Security Council Resolution 1373; the US Congress' International Money-Laundering Abatement and Anti-Terrorist Financing Act (2001); the Financial Aid Task Force (FATF)'s Eight Special Recommendations on Terrorist Finance established by the Group of Eight (G8); and cooperative initiatives by the EU, the Group of 7 (G7)'s Financial Stability Forum (FSF) and the Organisation for European Cooperation and Development (OECD). Lax or prohibitively secretive banking practices have been effectively curbed through both mandatory tightening and 'naming and shaming' and blacklisting by organisations like the FATF. Jurisdictions such as the Ukraine and Cyprus have overcome corruption. Smaller jurisdictions like the Bahamas, the Cayman Islands and Liechtenstein passed laws curbing the use of difficult-to-trace 'correspondent accounts'.

As of December 2003, however, terrorist assets frozen or seized had increased over the course of a year by only $23m, to $138m in total. This indicates that capacity building, better anti-corruption standards and controls, and enforcement of multilateral agreements is only part of the answer. Innovations such as banking 'white lists' and country boycotts by international financial institutions may make the money-laundering net finer.[30] Economic assistance that provides compliance incentives to countries whose liberal financial services have fuelled their economic growth could also help.[31] But there will remain opportunities for evasion for terrorist financiers.

Still a porous net

Greater scrutiny on the part of regulatory bodies, and by financial institutions themselves in the industrialised world, prompted al-Qaeda and its affiliates to look for funding channels to other, more irregular and increasingly local financial vehicles – including religious charities and hawala remittence systems – that are not subject to systematic regulation. In turn, as al-Qaeda has dispersed and come to rely more on local groups, such sources have also arguably become more efficient means of bankrolling terrorist operations. According to a US General Accounting Office report released in early December 2003, US officials still have no firm idea of how terrorists move their money, and the FBI – the lead US agency for tracking terrorist assets – still does not 'systematically collect or analyze' relevant information. In many cases, it is simply unable to do so.[32] Informal hawala remittance systems, for instance, require only the handshake agreement of two individuals in the source and the destination of the funds involved to effect a cash transfer between third parties in the different locales. The smaller the amount involved, the more likely it can be transferred by means of ready cash in hand, and the harder it is for a financial institution to detect and, therefore, record and report the transaction.

Terrorist operations are asymmetrically inexpensive. The Bali bombing cost under $35,000, the USS *Cole* operation about $50,000 and the 11 September attacks less than $500,000. Moving large amounts of cash therefore is not an operational necessity. Furthermore, since the Afghanistan intervention forced al-Qaeda to decentralise and eliminated the financial burden of maintaining a large physical base, al-Qaeda has needed less money to operate. Its increasing use of hawalas has prompted new laws in the US, Hong Kong and elsewhere requiring remittance houses to register. Compliance has been low, however. There are indications that al-Qaeda has converted its assets to gems (including 'conflict diamonds'), gold and other commodities including cigarettes, weapons and illicit drugs that are susceptible to bartering and hard to trace.[33]

Cooperation among financial authorities in the US, Europe and some Asian countries has been high, but Arab and other Muslim governments have been less forthcoming. Charitable giving is a basic element of Muslim piety.[34] In Saudi Arabia, richer companies and individuals are expected to pay 2.5% of their income for the welfare of the community. Islamic financial institutions are therefore less likely to scrutinise depositors presented as charities or charitable donors. In any event, governments in predominantly Muslim countries face domestic political constraints in imposing scrutiny on financial transactions. Inflows through charitable fronts and outflows from foreign sources remain difficult to monitor.

Much of al-Qaeda's funding comes from private donations of wealthy Saudis to apparent charities. In January 2002, Saudi Arabia announced that it was 'urgently implementing' a law to combat money-laundering by moving to freeze 150 suspect bank accounts, but provided no details. Private Saudi citizens have continued to provide 50–60% of Hamas's annual budget. Wealthy Saudis and others are still furnishing substantial support for madrassas throughout the Muslim world that indoctrinate and train jihadists, and to conservative Muslim schools in Western and Eastern Europe that potentially serve the same functions. After the May 2003 Riyadh bombings, however, Saudi cooperation in cracking down on terrorist financing intensified. Saudi authorities have placed strict controls on accounts held by charities, and these charities have been barred from making overseas wire transfers from their accounts. But there remain huge discrepancies between official Saudi and independent estimates of how much Saudis donate to charity and how much of that goes to overseas recipients. Outside sources puts the latter figure at over $6 billion, while the Saudi Ministry of Social Affairs cites $300–400m.[35] This gap suggests that a lack of Saudi vigilance could hinder the application of more stringent laws. In fact, while the new Saudi legal framework received the FATF's qualified approval in July 2004, the overall Saudi implementation effort was more critically assessed in the Council on Foreign Relations (CFR) Task Force on Terrorist Financing's second report in June 2004.

Some Arab countries have been more decisive in attacking the money-laundering problem on the regulatory level. The United Arab Emirates (UAE), through which at least $120,000 of the $500,000 advanced to the 11 September hijackers was channelled, for years showed little conviction in implementing financial controls and was among terrorist financiers' favourite jurisdictions due to its lax financial reporting standards and the absence of any requirement that financial institutions report cash deposits. UAE officials considered money-laundering primarily a phenomenon associated with drug-trafficking, uncommon in the Muslim country, and declined to crack down after the 1998 US embassy bombings in East Africa on the grounds that al-Qaeda funds used for criminal activities could not be distinguished from those used for what they deemed acceptable practices, such as training Islamic rebels in Bosnia-Herzegovina and Chechnya. Under US pressure, however, in January 2002, the UAE criminalised money laundering by imposing jail terms of up to seven years and fines as high as $82,000 on those transferring or depositing money in UAE accounts with the intent to conceal its origin. The UAE central bank was also empowered to exchange information on suspicious accounts with foreign counterparts, and all visitors were required to declare any funds in excess of $11,000 brought in from another country. Bahraini, Kuwaiti and Qatari authorities have similarly tightened their banking regulations. The UAE's failure to ratify the UN Convention for the Suppression of the Financing of Terrorism, however, exemplifies the hesitancy of many Muslim governments in undertaking permanent and binding international commitments to fight terrorist financing.

Transatlantic convergence has rendered some forms of terrorist funding more difficult – for instance, the EU in September 2003 joined the US in making Hamas's religious and charitable arms proscribed terrorist organisations, triggering blocks on donations. But funding from the Middle East/Gulf region, regardless of any new substantive statutory muscle, is likely to remain relatively unimpeded in the medium term.

Al-Qaeda is believed to have focused especially on Southeast Asia as an easy operating environment for fundraising, financing and money-laundering operations. In spite of the vigilance prompted by the Bali bombing and considerable counter-terrorism cooperation from several Southeast Asian governments, the funding of the Indonesian-based al-Qaeda affiliate JI has stayed abundant. This illustrates the stickiness of this problem. Hambali, who was arrested in August 2003, had $500,000 at his disposal for operations – a considerable amount, given how cheap terrorist operations are.[36] Hambali's assets, frozen in January 2003, and those of other al-Qaeda and JI operatives, came from eight sources:

- cash brought into the country by individuals
- 2% 'skim' from otherwise legitimate Islamic charities
- corporate conduits or fronts
- hawala remittances and gold sales
- direct contributions from JI members
- direct contributions from non-members
- established al-Qaeda accounts and investment vehicles, mainly in Islamic banks
- petty crime, racketeering, extortion, gunrunning and kidnapping

Despite the efforts of some Southeast Asian governments, law-enforcement in most areas is slack in the region.[37] Though money-laundering is prohibited in Thailand, $2.2bn in drug proceeds are laundered there annually, providing a ready illicit financial infrastructure for al-Qaeda to use. In March 2003, Thai authorities arrested 25 Arab men suspected of money-laundering and forging travel documents for al-Qaeda. Money-laundering is not even a criminal offence in Myanmar, and was made illegal in the Philippines and Indonesia only in 2001 and 2002, respectively; all three remain blacklisted by the FATF.

Charitable giving is encouraged by some Muslim governments – in late 2002, Indonesia made it tax-deductible. Southeast Asian diasporas are important sources of funds. Those in Arab countries, like the Muslims among Filipino guest workers in Saudi Arabia, may be subject to intensified radicalisation, and consequently keener to support militant Muslim causes at home. Conversely, resident Southeast Asians, who are already radicalised, travel and win converts and contributions among Muslims now living in the host countries. In the 1990s, for example, radical Indonesian clerics Abdullah Sungkar and Abu Bakar Bashir raised large amounts of money by way of sermons and audiotape sales from Indonesian exiles in Australia. Money from overseas can easily be transferred to local parties through hawalas. The World Bank and the IMF estimate that in 2000 hawala remittances constituted 5% of the Philippines' total private incoming transfers (which totalled $6bn), 21% of Indonesia's and 50% of Pakistan's.[38] Such nations' economic dependence on informal remittances makes them reluctant to crack down on hawala systems. In any case, informal remittances are ideally suited for circumventing currency controls (which Malaysia employs) and eluding the region's weak banking systems. Among the other operational virtues of hawala transactions are that they are quick, leave only a scant and opaque data trail (often couched in code-words), involve no physical movement of cash, and can involve 'cut-outs' that shield ultimate sources and recipients of funds.[39]

Southeast Asian regimes also appear to be broadly incapable of corralling more conventional and formal disguised al-Qaeda investment vehicles. Beyond the limitations of regional legal systems, the Saudi Arabian government's political and economic leverage has also made it difficult for Southeast Asian governments to shut down branch offices of the Saudi government-funded Islamic International Relief Organisation (IIRO). In the Philippines, for instance, the IIRO funnelled money to bin Laden's Lebanese brother-in-law, Mohammad Jammal Khalifa, who had set up IIRO outposts that funded arms purchases and other logistical requirements for Abu Sayyaf and the MILF from the late 1980s until the mid-1990s. Philippines intelligence could not shut it down for six years owing to Riyadh's threats of terminating the work visas of several hundred thousand Filipino guest workers. Even when the Philippines IIRO office was finally closed in 1995, its operations and staff were simply taken over by another Islamic charity, the Islamic Wisdom Worldwide Mission, headed by a close Khalifa associate. Until 11 September 2001, IIRO offices in Indonesia and Malaysia stayed open and funded projects in the Philippines as well as their host countries.[40]

Globalising financial counter-terrorism standards
The theoretical requirements of corralling terrorist finance are relatively unambiguous and well-captured by the FATF's Eight Recommendations. Those recommendations are:

• ratify and implement UN instruments

- criminalise the financing of terrorism and associated money-laundering
- freeze and confiscate terrorist assets
- report suspicious transactions related to terrorism
- formalise greater international cooperation through treaties or other agreements
- license and register businesses engaged in alternative forms of remittance
- require accurate and meaningful originator data for wire transfers
- review the adequacy of laws regulating non-profit organisations

But the FATF comprises only 33 member-states. As of December 2003, only 83 of the 191 countries that the UN required under Security Council Resolution 1373 to submit reports on terrorist financing had complied. US and UN officials know the whereabouts of only a small fraction of the 272 individuals named by the UN as sponsors of terrorism. Thus, the recommendations raise the question of how to persuade and enable non-Western jurisdictions to apply stricter controls. Even if fully implemented, a UN instrument such as the 1999 UN International Convention for the Suppression of the Financing of Terrorism would be essentially toothless since the UN Counter-Terrorism Committee has no power to sanction non-compliers.[41] Where they are most needed, criminalisation, seizure, more rigorous reporting and registration standards, and stiffer charity regulation require statutory and administrative changes to which governments may often be culturally resistant. Treaties, even if attainable, could be hard to enforce for the same reason.

The initial mobilisation against terrorist financing following the 11 September attacks has resulted in tightened mandatory and voluntary regulatory regimes and improved enforcement that has substantially denied al-Qaeda access to Western financial institutions. The FATF itself has indicated that regulating mainstream Western financial institutions is no longer a big problem.[42] Perhaps the most important measure that Western governments and regulators can yet take is to further tighten controls on charities by adding them to official lists of terrorist organisations and, correspondingly, freezing their assets. Hawala money-transfer schemes and Islamic charities whose operations are partially legitimate, however, cannot be completely eliminated. The availability of hawala operations and the existence of dual-purpose Muslim charities make any banking system vulnerable provided the fact that the customers using them are terrorist abettors remains unknown. Although political and economic pressure has produced useful legal reforms in Arab countries as well as South and Southeast Asia, implementation remains a serious problem. As with other forms of counter-terrorism cooperation, the main impediment is countervailing domestic pressure on the governments in question not to kowtow to major powers – particularly the US – that are seen as anti-Muslim.

Wholesale success in thwarting economic support for terrorism therefore is likely to turn, as do most improvements in counter-terrorism, on advances in intelligence cooperation and information exchange about individual and corporate depositors. In its first report in October 2002, the CFR Task Force counselled the creation of an international organisation dedicated exclusively to combating terrorist finance. The organisation would facilitate multilateral initiatives to set international standards for charitable organisations and hawalas, compose 'white lists' as well as blacklists, facilitate inter-governmental intelligence sharing on terrorist groups and their means of support, arrange technical assistance (through the IMF and World Bank) for countries in need of it and formulate IMF conditionality guidelines aimed at curtailing terrorist financing.[43] The advent of such an organisation would constitute a positive step towards strengthening and harmonising financial counter-terrorism standards throughout the world – in particular, by concentrating diplomatic pressure onto non-compliant states. Material improvements via any new institutional mechanism, however, are likely to take years to arise.

In the meantime, pressure imposed bilaterally will probably be the best way to get results. As the CFR Task Force implicitly recognised in designating the plurality of its prescriptions 'Recommendations Applicable to the United States', the US, owing to superior financial resources, military power, and intelligence and law-enforcement capabilities, has the most leverage. One of its most effective tools is the US State Department's official List of Foreign Terrorist Organizations. Inclusion on the list makes foreign terrorist organisations (FTOs) liable to presidentially authorised blocking orders that bar the designated organisation from raising or distributing funds in the US. Promulgation of the list apprises other jurisdictions of Washington's negative assessment, and puts them on notice that permissive policies vis-à-vis those organisations could trigger unfavourable US treatment.

This alone is not enough. The US also needs to make greater diplomatic efforts to persuade Western governments to tighten controls on charitable and political 'wings' of terrorist groups by adding them to their lists and, correspondingly, freezing their assets. The US position is that the fungibility of money makes such wings indistinguishable from operational ones for purposes of imposing financial restrictions, so the US tends to include both on its list. The EU, which publishes its own list, has been slower to do so. But since 11 September, the EU list has converged on the United States' list, and in September 2003, after years of US and Israeli importuning, Brussels included Hamas's political and charitable arms on the EU list. This may signal general European recognition of what former FBI analyst Matthew Levitt has called 'the myth of the 'wings'.[44] Follow-up may remain a problem. Three weeks later, the United Kingdom's Charity Commission unfroze the assets of one of Hamas's largest charitable fronts.[45]

Europe–US disharmony, while not trivial, is manageable due to appreciable institutional capacities, converging threat perceptions and thick bilateral relationships. A comparable concord with some non-European states, especially Muslim ones, will be harder to build. For example, the Haramain Charitable Foundation, a Saudi Arabia-based organisation implicated in financing al-Qaeda that has raised up to $30m a year, was required to suspend all activities in Saudi Arabia in 2003, but it remained active in other countries by virtue of direct private contributions from local Muslims as well as citizens of Saudi Arabia and other Gulf states, and opened a school in Indonesia in late 2003.[46] Haramain was finally dissolved by Saudi authorities in mid-2004, when Riyadh announced plans to put Saudi-based charities under government control. More diplomatic pressure, artfully applied, is required to ensure that Riyadh follows through and other Muslim countries follow suit. Stylistically, the preferred approach would be intense behind-the-scenes dialogue, enhanced by various economic and political incentives. Carrots could include technical assistance and perhaps implied linkages to US trade concessions. Sticks might include the three official lists that the US government publishes – of terrorist organisations, jurisdictions 'of concern' and state sponsors of terrorism. These should be used in a judicious, graduated and reasonably quiet manner: their bite rests in actual or potential commercial disadvantage, not public humiliation. Other governments and regional organisations should also be encouraged to publish similar lists themselves.

The Secretary of the Treasury's new power, under the USA PATRIOT Act, to designate foreign jurisdictions or financial institutions as being 'of primary money-laundering concern' could be diplomatically useful. Any jurisdiction so designated is liable to 'special measures' short of blocking orders (such as severing correspondent relationships between offending foreign and American institutions) that do not require presidential authorisation. In 2002, the CFR Task Force exhorted the Treasury Secretary to make use of this power.[47] In addition, he could cast any jurisdiction as one 'of concern' if a designated FTO is known to raise or deposit funds there but has not been penalised by that jurisdiction. The implicit threat would be to include exceptionally recalcitrant states on the US State Department's official list of state-sponsors of terrorism. This option would naturally be subject to political constraints. For example, Washington would be unlikely to designate Pakistan – an important and on balance helpful counter-terrorism partner – as being 'of concern' for failing to completely choke off Laskar-e Jhangvi or Laskar-e Toiba (both formally banned in Pakistan, and FTOs) in light of Musharraf's tenuous domestic position vis-à-vis Islamists. But in other cases, this kind of pressure could not only improve enforcement with respect to conventional financial vehicles but prompt regulatory innovations for isolating assets placed in less conventional ones. Indeed, establishing a better surveillance regime for irregular means of holding and transferring assets is one of the most important hurdles for the global counter-terrorism coalition to clear.

Chapter 3

Social Science and Diplomacy

Diplomatic pressure on vulnerable countries like Indonesia and Kenya and deepened bilateral intelligence and law-enforcement links – aspects of hard power – are necessary, but in the long term insufficient. Major powers also need to address the deeper causes of Islamist terrorism. Most measures aimed mainly at advancing counter-terrorist enforcement and prevention capabilities do not do so. Western and regional governments, of course, do need to attend urgently to immediate 'hard' counter-terrorism concerns such as law-enforcement and intelligence cooperation. But ultimately, to defeat a resilient, religiously motivated adversary, they must also look beyond them and continue supporting gradual political and economic reform, paying especially close attention to cushioning the impact of protracted deprivation on those ordinary citizens who provide the mass base for Islamic political groups and militias. This kind of culturally transformative counter-terrorism involves primarily the application of soft power. It is a politically delicate and fraught process.

Underwriting political and economic reforms that produce civil mechanisms for addressing political grievances that have been transmogrified into religious imperatives is the programmatic solution to the problem of root causes. The tough question is how this should be done in particular circumstances. Since al-Qaeda's leadership has grievances that are not readily negotiable, overt conflict resolution is not an option for taming the group. Instead, beyond decimating its existing hardcore ranks through law-enforcement, intelligence and military action, the prime objective must be to deprive it of recruits. A key early step in that direction is figuring out what motivates potential terrorists.

Islamist motivations

Little headway has been made in understanding precisely what makes al-Qaeda recruits tick – and, consequently, in figuring out how to shrink the terrorist talent pool. Estimates of al-Qaeda's wider constituency of peripheral supporters and sympathisers range from tens of thousands to millions of Muslims (depending on the breadth of one's definitions of 'support' and 'sympathy'). In the Gulf and wider Arab world, poverty does not seem to be a major factor in terrorist motivations. The 11 September hijackers came largely from middle-class to upper-middle-class roots. Most were from Saudi Arabia, which has a relatively high per-capita income and qualifies as a middle-class country. Indeed, given the home economics of many Arab societies, the poorest young men would be unlikely to be sent to madrassas for indoctrination or to training camps for learning terrorist skills due to pressure to stay at home and help the family subsist. Lack of education and overt maladjustment also do not correlate closely with terrorism. The 11 September hijackers were well educated and grew up in relative domestic stability. They had shown no striking signs of psychological disturbance or abnormality. The new terrorist does not appear to be inherently joyless or depressed. Bin Laden himself hosted cookouts in Sudan in the mid-1990s, where his recruits played soccer, rode horses and enthusiastically socialised. Several of the 11 September hijackers enjoyed drinking and strip clubs.

Yet it would be a mistake to dismiss poverty as a contributing cause of terrorism. It is likely that the 11 September hijackers were in part vicariously inspired by the relative deprivation of many of their Muslim brothers. Material deprivation may be a more direct and potent trigger in other parts of the Muslim world, such as Southeast Asia and East Africa. In Indonesia, in particular, the poor economic performance of the state since the late 1990s seems to coincide with the growth of radical Islam in general and in particular the heightened aggression of Jemaah Islamiah. Most Islamist militants in Turkey come from poor backgrounds, as do left-wing and Kurdish separatist insurgents in that country. The weakness or failure of state structures – usually coincident with poverty – have also led individuals to turn towards radical Islamic groups with terrorist connections, such as al-Ittihad al-Islamiah in Somalia. While this does not necessarily or even usually translate into terrorist activity, a broader pattern of social, economic and political marginalisation – which may include relative poverty – appears relevant to generating terrorist motivations.

The absence of democracy looks to be an acutely important engine of terrorism. Authoritarian regimes in Muslim countries – particularly Saudi Arabia and Egypt, the respective homelands of bin Laden and second-in-command Ayman al-Zawahiri – deprive their citizens of a sense of participation in defining their own future. Two additional phenomena have amplified this problem. One is flatter economic expectations brought about by a combination of rapid population growth and relatively low oil prices. Even oil-rich rentier states like Saudi Arabia, where real per-capita GDP has declined by more than half in the past 20 years, can no longer calm their citizens with money. Political and economic conditions in Muslim countries yield dashed hopes, which produces a general sense of 'anomie' – sociologist Emile Durkheim's term meaning a personal state of isolation and anxiety owing to a breakdown of the state's mechanisms of social organisation.

The natural result might be lethargy rather than violence. Tipping the balance is the rhetorical power of bin Laden's virulent accusation that the ruling elites of these countries are apostate in their disrespect for the most pious elements of society and in their close relationships with Western governments. He and al-Qaeda's chief propagandists attribute relatively low material expectations and political decadence to impious governments under the evil influence and domination of America and its Western partners, thus completing the circuit from obscure unhappiness to terrorist impulse. Young, dissatisfied Muslims receptive to this message conclude that an Islamist revolt would improve their lot, personally empower them and vindicate their religion and culture, and the past futility of political Islam at the national level in the Gulf makes bin Laden's global approach the logical outlet. The forcible occupation of Iraq by US-led, mainly Christian nations, at least in the short term, has strengthened this line of reasoning by bolstering bin Laden's claims that the US intends to loot Arab oil and dominate the politics of the Middle East and Gulf. An eventual independent democratic Iraqi state, however, could weaken the case for radicalisation.

Domestic policies

In the United States, the 11 September attacks made immigration a national-security issue. The hijackers had valid visas for entering the US. More broadly, the 48 radical Islamists implicated in terrorist plots in the US between 1993 and 2001 all used legal immigration devices – student, tourist and business visas, green cards, amnesty and asylum – to get into the country.[1] Although the United States' massive illegal immigration problem diverts resources from counter-terrorism, this factor was not critical. Rather, the lack of coordination – especially in data-sharing – among the CIA, FBI, INS and State Department was the principal cause of the security failure that allowed the hijackers to penetrate the intelligence and law-enforcement net. Since 11 September, improved data-sharing and aviation security and the consolidation of national-security functions (both structurally and operationally) have begun to address key vulnerabilities.

There are substantially fewer Muslims in the US than in Europe, and their assimilation of American values and integration into American society has been relatively successful owing to its history as a 'melting pot'. Thus, assimilation and integration are generally more thoroughgoing among American Muslims than European ones.[2] But American Muslims' perception of anti-Muslim bias in post-11 September law enforcement and their growing conviction that the US has overreached in Iraq and ignored the plight of the Palestinians have alienated a significant number of American Muslims. Furthermore, the interrogation of Khalid Shaikh Mohammed, the captured al-Qaeda director of global operations, has revealed that al-Qaeda's US strategy involves recruiting homegrown assets – US citizens (especially African-American Muslims) or other Western passport holders. In turn, African-American converts have made Islam the fastest-growing religion in the US. The US Muslim population, then, has probably become more susceptible to radicalisation.

Yet European Muslims may be even more susceptible. Operationally, Europe has proven useful to al-Qaeda as a platform for attacking the US and, as the US has firmed up homeland defence, now constitutes a proxy target. Traditionally, Muslim agitation in European countries has emanated from political problems that the diaspora fled in their home countries. Thus, for instance, each of France's seven Muslim organisations is financially and ideologically linked to a different, substantially Muslim foreign country.[3] Within European host countries, though, Muslims are generally economically and socially marginalised, politically under-represented and less literate than most other social groups.[4] With the exception of France and lately Germany, European governments have not encouraged assimilation, eschewing the American 'melting pot' approach. Olivier Roy has noted that the radical impulse among European Muslims is increasingly based not on traditionally parochial or geographically circumscribed 'diaspora' grievances about the struggles of their brethren in their homelands, but on the perceived disrespect and injustice visited on them by host peoples and governments.

Thus, the objectives of radical European Muslims are becoming more and more 'universalised'.[5] Lack of assimilation or integration in Europe has reinforced broader religiously based distaste for Western modernity. Historically, Muslims residing in Western countries who experience such revulsion have directed their rebellious instincts homeward, in coercive attempts to reform Westernised Arab governments. Sayyid Qutb's disgust with an America that seemed licentious, racist, overly fond of Israel and culturally barren helped impel him to join the Muslim Brotherhood and violently challenge Gamal Abdel Nasser's secular rule in Egypt. Currently, with domestic Islamist movements having been defeated by authoritarian Arab states, disaffected Arab expatriates instead join bin Laden's expansive global jihad. Studying in Germany, 11 September ringleader Muhammad Atta, like Qutb an Egyptian, came to loathe Western modernity and to resent its worldly temptations. But he bypassed Cairo in favour of New York and Washington. The US-led intervention in Iraq has, at least in the short term, fuelled radicalisation.[6] Operationally, this means that radical European Muslims are inclined to carry their fight to wherever fellow Muslims appear to be imperilled or besieged. For example, two men with British passports – both of whom lived in the UK, one of whom was born there – were involved in a suicide bombing in Israel in May 2003.

Hard security alone can at best contain the threat of transnational Islamist terrorism in Europe. Moreover, containment in Europe will become more difficult. European Muslims have appreciably higher fertility rates than non-Muslim Europeans, and the continent's need for imported labour is likely to be filled in considerable part by Muslims from nearby states in the Greater Middle East. Thus, the Muslim share of Europe's population will grow.

This means that, other things being equal, hard counter-terrorism resources will be all the more strained.

Structurally, however, Europe has the mature and sophisticated governmental institutions required to implement the ambitious social policies that are probably required to reach an accommodation with the 15m Muslims within the pre-enlargement EU. The glibly theoretical solution is a roughly even blend of assimilation and integration along American lines. Assimilation is statutorily enshrined in France and Germany, which require naturalised citizens to meet minimum standards of national language competence and cultural knowledge. Comparably rigorous requirements have been lacking in the UK. At the same time, a relatively large number of high-profile Muslims in media and intellectual circles indicates an appreciable level of integration in Britain. Muslims are also quite well represented in local (though not in national) government in the UK. Nevertheless, well before 11 September French commentators and counter-terrorism analysts sardonically dubbed London 'Londonistan'. There are identifiable reasons for Britain's proclivity to spawn radical Muslims. The bulk of Britain's Muslims are from South Asia – mainly Pakistan – and were raised in the Sunni Deobandi tradition. This sect of Islam arose in predominantly Hindu areas of India, and emphasises strict adherence to Islamic laws and customs as a means of preserving Islam against outside influences.[7]

Furthermore, reflexive 'politically correct' multiculturalism – which has manifested itself as, for instance, the failure of the UK to enforce the requirement of the British Nationality Act of 1981 that applicants for citizenship have 'sufficient' knowledge of the English, Welsh or Scottish Gaelic languages – has perversely discouraged Muslims from learning the ways of their new countries, thus isolating them from the mainstream and stoking radicalisation. The upshot is that in Britain, groups that have insular inclinations to begin with have become even more so. This shows that just as assimilation alone does not moderate anti-Western feelings among Muslims, integration alone does not do so either. Instead, it appears to shift political attention from the national to the religious, reinforcing the universalisation of Muslim grievances that Roy has identified. In enacting more exacting language and cultural requirements in 2004 for new entrants, however, the UK has taken steps to remedy the problem.

France, the archetypal 'civic nation', strictly applies its language and culture naturalisation standards, requires that French be spoken at official events, and rigidly enforces the separation of church and state. In theory, France, which wants its 5m Muslims to think of themselves as French, might seem a good model. To match stiff assimilation standards, there is a high degree of institutional integration. Muslim citizens of France, like those of any other European country, enjoy the same government entitlements as everyone else. Public education is free, university registration very cheap. Yet radicalisation has been thriving in France as well as the UK.[8] Stringent assimilation requirements – such as France's prohibiting Muslim girls from wearing headscarves in schools in late 2003 – can have an exclusionary and alienating effect. Of roughly 1,000 imams in France, only 9% are French citizens. However assimilated and integrated they may seem, many second-generation French Muslims of North African lineage have contempt for the French state because they perceive (and, in fact, receive) disdain from mainstream French people.

The absence of attitudinal integration, then, trumps more superficial forms of acceptance. Australian journalist Sarah Turnbull, long a French resident, notes that 'in France "multiculturalism" is pretty much a dirty word'. She adds that 'the French cling stubbornly to the idea that theirs is a white nation' and that 'culture is viewed as an established entity that must be preserved and protected from foreign influences'.[9] This means that Arab Muslim assimilation is not repaid by a welcoming attitude in French political and professional circles: 'compared to say America, England and Australia, immigrants in France are startlingly absent from high-profile, public life. Despite the great wave of migration during the fifties and sixties, there are no North African or black news readers on television, for example'.[10] France's lesson is that state-imposed assimilation devoid of any complementary parity in social and political status effected through integration is insufficient to contain radicalism and, worse still, can produce cultural blowback.

It is salutary that the trend Europe-wide, as well as in the UK and France, is towards enhancing and equalising assimilative and integrative social mechanisms.[11] As noted earlier, a signature aspect of European integration as currently defined is open borders within the union. A key European value is a sense of civic community.

These factors undergird an emerging European consensus that emphasises both immigrants' duties (adapting to new languages, laws, customs and restraints) and their rights (religious freedom, free speech, women's rights and citizenship). Though criticised by orthodox and progressive French Muslims alike as a potential source of marginalisation, the new government-endorsed French Council for the Muslim Religion is intended to help secure a position for Muslims in the civic mainstream and produce an indigenous, moderate version of Islam. The Muslim Council of Britain has similar integrative potential, but requires complementary assimilative measures to become a leading vehicle for Muslim social and political advancement. There remains considerable uncertainty among European jurisdictions about whether suppressing or ignoring radical Muslim clerics is more likely to depress radicalisation and jihadist recruitment.[12] Whichever policy is adopted, it is incomplete. Thoroughly 'mainstreaming' Muslims will probably call for more aggressive and controversial policies. These include affirmative action and government subsidies for moderate Islamic schools.[13]

There are identifiable potential remedies close at hand. Within the UK, the most rigorous fair employment laws in Europe, verging on affirmative action, are in effect in Northern Ireland.[14] Workers there are entitled to damages even if they have been only indirectly and unintentionally discriminated against. Such provisions, though often resented by the Protestant majority, have helped close the Catholic–Protestant employment gap in Northern Ireland and have almost certainly kept some young Catholics from joining the IRA. Positive discrimination in police recruitment, in particular, doubled the Catholic proportion of officers in the Police Service of Northern Ireland over the course of two years. More affirmative encouragement of moderate Islam, however, would be much less likely to do so. This notion clashes with another cherished European standard – the removal of religion from public political discourse – and with general suspicion of 'faith schools'. But the fact is that the global jihad has inexorably invested both international and domestic politics with religious content. For a government to restrict its own capacity to ameliorate the terrorism problem on account of rigid adherence to church/state separation would be obtuse and counter-productive. Focused government subsidies for Muslim schools that follow a moderate form of Islam, for instance, would be salutary. Britain has begun to extend limited subsidies to Muslim schools, but has made no effort to encourage moderate Islamic education as opposed to fundamentalism, whose support by wealthy Wahhabi Muslims gives it a substantial competitive advantage. France might reconsider making an exception to its strict policy of separation of church and state with respect to public funding of religious schools. Some have even suggested that European governments fund the education of local imams in the interest of diluting the insulating connections between diaspora and conservative clerics from their countries of origin and of supplying community leaders who speak the host country's language with a better understanding of the social challenges facing Muslims in Europe.[15] The government funding of mosques – with certain conditions – should be examined more incisively.

To further ease integration, finance ministers should attune themselves to financial and commercial needs that are peculiar to Muslims. To take a modest example: by exempting certain co-ownership schemes from the requirement of paying a double stamp duty, the UK budget encouraged the creation of a joint Arab Banking Corporation and Bristol & West mortgage facility for Muslims whereby they would not have to pay interest directly to a lender – which contravenes the sharia – but instead would co-own property with Bristol & West and gradually buy out its share. Such devices enable more Muslims to own residential and commercial property. More direct government measures – such as special subsidies for businesses operated by Muslims – would risk negative reactions from sections of the white population, which in Britain showed itself willing to indulge in racially motivated violence in riots in the northern 'mill and mosque' towns of Oldham (Muslim population: 25,000, or 11%), Burnley (Muslim population: 8,000, or 8%) and Bradford (Muslim population: 82,750, or 17%) in spring and summer 2001. But some initial tension may be a cost worth bearing: a palpably benevolent outreach from the state to the Muslim population would be broadly conducive to increased Muslim participation in politics – a linchpin of successful assimilation and integration.

European governments also need to determine whether expanded or curtailed immigration has the most ameliorative effect on Islamic radicalism. This is a difficult question, as integrative considerations tend to favour expansion, assimilative ones curtailment. Thus, the UK and France have tended to take different tacks.

British officials worry that reducing immigration will weaken social cohesion, and instead favour heightening the surveillance and monitoring of Muslim communities and encouraging them to provide useful information and intelligence. But their French counterparts are more concerned about the negative effect that large influxes of immigrants has on assimilation. Yet France needs foreign labour to sustain acceptable economic growth, and therefore is constrained as to how much it can restrict immigration. Accordingly, both countries need efficient procedures and safeguards for filtering out those who would be most likely to fuel radicalism. The UK has sought to tighten its asylum policy without capping the aggregate number of immigrants. France, for its part, eased quantitative limits on immigration in early 2003 while establishing greater selectivity through US-style quotas.

On a grander social and political scale, given Arab sensitivities to US pressure – particularly following American military intervention in Iraq – it may make sense for Europe to draw some political heat away from the US in any renewed effort to forge a solution to the Israeli–Palestinian conflict by assuming a more prominent mediating role.[16] The EU derives credibility with Islamic countries (including Iraq) on account of their mutual economic dependence and Brussels' support for the Palestinian Authority. This enhances EU financial leverage. That, in turn, would increase if the EU revived the 27-member European-Mediterranean Partnership, which was established in 1995 with high hopes of deepening ties among the countries of the Mediterranean but became enervated because of the second Palestinian intifada and 11 September.

Muslim perceptions and US Middle East policy

Negative Muslim perceptions of the United States make controversial but largely non-optional US policies in the Middle East, the Gulf and the wider Muslim world all the more difficult to execute. Immediately after 11 September, the Qatar-based satellite television station al-Jazeera resolutely portrayed Muslims as victims of a 'crusade' in Afghanistan – a term initially and unfortunately used by the Bush administration itself in characterising the intervention – rather than culprits in the attacks that necessitated a self-defensive US-led intervention against the Taliban and al-Qaeda. The network also manifested a kind of cognitive dissonance, championing bin Laden as a righteous defender of Islam (and showing his inflammatory videotapes) while denying his involvement in the attacks that bestowed that status. The effect of such coverage may not have been all bad: it eased the tension of Muslim viewers as some Arab governments, including that of Qatar itself, aided the US in its campaign against terrorism. But moderate voices that might have changed popular attitudes were overwhelmed.

Al-Jazeera chose to broadcast more radical figures and the Saudi government and media, in particular, denounced the 'war on terror' as an attack on Islam as a whole. Gulf newspapers construed President Bush's characterisation of Iran and Iraq as part of an 'axis of evil' in his January 2002 State of the Union Address as a declaration of war against any opponent of Israeli aggression, despite the fact that North Korea was included in the axis. Egypt's semi-official newspaper *Al-Ahram* – which is hardly revolutionary in tone – read in the speech 'good motives for some to continue with terrorism'. Before the 2003 Iraq war, the Arab press had roundly written off Saddam Hussein as a loser as well as a tyrant stripped bare by the 1990–91 Gulf War and the sanctions regime and too weak to threaten his neighbours. Thus, Muslim media outlets did not buy American and British assertions that Iraq had WMD, and cast the military intervention as revenge against Muslims generally for 11 September and a pretext for oil-motivated US imperialism. In any case, Arabs view as hypocritical Washington's tacit approval of an undeclared Israeli nuclear capability next to its overt condemnation of a Muslim nation's developing nuclear weapons.[17] The unexpected strength of the indigenous but jihadist-assisted Iraqi insurgency has also strained relations between Islam and the West by prompting US and British troops to continue to inflict heavy Iraqi casualties, many of them civilian non-combatants. And the revelations of extreme and systematic American abuses of Iraqi prisoners in Abu Ghraib prison has become an emblem of American hypocrisy for Muslims, and driven Muslim perceptions of the United States government and of Americans to a new low.

The Iraq war has also had some countervailing, though far from completely offsetting, effects. For one, the war caused transnational Islamic terrorists to refocus on the Gulf.[18] Literally and figuratively, this brought terrorism home to Arab populations.

The Riyadh bombing in May 2003 killed 35 Saudis. Subsequently, the Saudi media – with the blessing of parts of the regime – have openly acknowledged the religious, social and political roots of terrorism in some Wahhabi Muslim practices. In *al-Watan*, a liberal daily, Adel Zaid al-Tarifi wrote that Friday sermons include 'elements of religious fanaticism'. Raid Qusi commented in Arab News that media's 'the see-no-evil, hear-no-evil, speak-no-evil' stance would no longer fool the Saudi people or the international community. While the Saudi interior ministry has limited tolerance for such confessional open-mindedness, it has triggered more soul-searching elsewhere in the Muslim world.[19] Although virtually all Arab media characterise Palestinian suicide attacks as 'martyrdom operations', terrorism is now discussed more openly and, in many cases, as the strategic threat that it is.

On balance, the counter-terrorism coalition faces a Muslim world whose populations have become more anti-Western by virtue of the Iraq intervention, but whose governments as well as populations are also more cognisant of genuine terrorist threats. There are tentative indications that the Bush administration understands both the urgent need to improve America's image among Muslims and the limited opportunities for doing so. In September 2003, the White House-appointed US Advisory Group on Public Diplomacy for the Arab and Muslim World – chaired by Edward Djerejian, a former US ambassador to Syria of Arab and Armenian descent – issued a report entitled 'Changing Minds, Winning Peace'. The report recommended a substantial increase in the $150m that the US government spent on public diplomacy in the Arab and Muslim world, which reflected a drop from the early 1990s of nearly 50% in real terms. The document also noted that most of that amount went to exchange programmes, overhead and salaries, and only $25m to outreach programmes. More broadly, the panel stressed that mere 'spin' was insufficient, alluding to the Bush administration's series of glib, naively perky television commercials – suspended after several Arab countries refused to show them – purporting to highlight 'shared values' and show that Muslims in the US were accorded dignity and equal rights. Senior State Department officials were impressed with the report.[20] Jeffrey Gedmin and Craig Kennedy, two Americans at the helms of think-tanks in Europe, wrote of American diplomacy in Europe:

Unlike the marketing campaigns of Phillip Morris, the pri-
mary goal of U.S. public diplomacy cannot be merely 'to sell'
the product of American foreign policy; it must offer explana-
tions of, and facilitate open debate about, the ideas underpin-
ning those policies. This kind of approach represents the
United States at its best and gives Americans the best chance
to persuade others of a particular policy's merits.[21]

Applying this prescription to US diplomacy in the Muslim world is far more important.

The substance of US policies, insofar as they will inevitably involve support for Israel and maintaining substantial leverage in the Gulf, is perhaps inherently liable to alienate large numbers of Muslims. Better public diplomacy in explaining those policies is no substitute for executing them in ways that more directly improve Muslim lives and alleviate Muslim suspicions.[22] The Middle East/Gulf region poses the stiffest challenge. A relatively uncontroversial consensus has emerged that the US-led coalition should aim to reform illiberal Arab partners politically and economically. Political repression in Saudi Arabia and Egypt has defeated attempts by political Islam to radicalise states, but it has also exported, and indeed helped to transnationalise, terrorism. Fifteen of the 19 hijackers of 11 September were Saudi, and the ringleader, Muhammad Atta, was Egyptian. Absent a new political and economic dispensation, demographic pressures from rising and increasingly youthful and rebellious populations, declining per-capita GDP and non-participatory political systems may merely portend export growth in terrorists.

Over the longer term, these structural factors will begin to change the character of Middle Eastern societies in ways that will make US–Arab relations even harder to manage for both sides. Between 2001 and 2015, the population in the region (including Iran) is estimated to rise from 304m to 400m. The 2–5% population growth rates responsible for this enormous increase will keep the population relatively young, which correlates with political violence. High growth rates also practically mandate low or negative GDP growth, and, without substantial government intervention, would help perpetuate the low status of women, a low standard of living and low literacy rates. As some Middle Eastern governments try to placate Islamist pressure groups by permitting the continuation of restrictions on the role of women in their societies, these high birth rates will continue. At the same time, deteriorating educational systems will constrain literacy growth and declining per-capita GDP will be reflected in lower standards of living. According to the World Bank, real per-capita income in the Middle East and North Africa fell by 2% per year between 1985 and 1995 – the largest decline in any developing region in the world.

Even as these ominous demographic changes are taking place, loading weak and increasingly poor states in competition for oil and water with a disproportionately large cohort of unemployable, frustrated young men, thanks to the advances in information technology and freer speech political consciousness in the region will grow as options for ruling elites shrink. The burden of coping with these developments rests on both sides. For Arab leaders, the goal must be to build domestic institutions for promoting capital and labour mobility, while permitting greater pluralism. For the US and its allies, as well as multilateral institutions, the goal should be to increase foreign assistance aimed at those who are most disadvantaged by economic and technological change, and to develop infrastructure and institutions that will attract investment. Technical assistance will be needed as well, to help demographically besieged countries develop effective health care, environment and education policies. To support these efforts, the US and its major-power partners will need to invest more heavily in promoting Arab-language, Middle Eastern and Islamic studies to increase the supply of Westerners who can operate comfortably and effectively in the Muslim world.

In the near-to-medium term, the overall relationship between the United States and its Western partners, on one hand, and the Arab world and Iran, on the other, will be shaped by the Israeli–Palestinian dispute; post-conflict developments with respect to Iraq; the degree of American dependence on Saudi energy; and restrictions on the ability of regional states to cooperate openly with the US due to popular support for bin Laden's cause. Another major factor will be the degree to which the successful suppression of terrorist movements in the region leads to the export of terrorism to the US. Trade, which tends to thicken connections between and among states, is likely to grow only in the energy sector. Otherwise, commerce will remain limited between the US and the region, as it is within the region itself.

Outside the energy sector, US investment in the region will be constrained by fear of instability, terrorism, intrusive state sectors, byzantine regulation, underdeveloped banking sectors and fragile physical infrastructure.

In this light, meeting the demands of transformative counter-terrorism will require significant departures from current practices by both Western and Muslim governments. The industrialised nations devote less than 0.25% of their aggregate gross national product to foreign assistance; the United States, at 0.1% until 2001, has been one of the least generous. In March 2002, in Monterrey, Mexico, President Bush announced that he would seek to increase the US foreign assistance budget by 50% by 2006. Arab governments, for their part, have brutally repressed regime-challenging Islamist groups but at the same time acquiesced in anti-Western, often Islamist, sentiment and propaganda to release popular pressure resulting from their partnerships with Western powers. In Saudi Arabia, since 11 September, Crown Prince Abdullah has been exhorting religious educators to emphasise Islam's tolerance, and has appeared to understand that Saudi Arabia would be better off democratising and that Saudi schools must better equip the country's youth with practical skills that will make them more employable and build human capital to power economic prosperity.

Educational exchange programmes can be valuable, but if not executed properly can end up confirming negative perceptions of American culture and society, as in the case of Sayyid Qutb. To minimise this risk, exchange programmes should ideally target the technocratic and academic elite. The US also has to explain itself better to conservative Islam in the hope of keeping it from falling into the radical camp. At the same time, the US must better appreciate the need for subtlety in its communications with Muslim populations. Attempting to force modernity on a population that is in many respects pre-modern can backfire. Aggressively encouraging Muslim women not to wear the veil, for example, has been received by many Muslims – women as well as men – as ham-handed colonialist entrepreneurship and propaganda. Fresh-faced ingenuousness will not work, either, as the State Department's failed advertising campaign showed.

US initiatives should initially be small-scale 'incubators of democratic values' that could be enhanced on the basis of measurable success, lessons learned, availability of resources and the specific circumstances of the countries from which visitors might come.[23] American education remains perhaps the most respected US institution in Islam.[24] But American universities in the Middle East have been under-funded and unable to offer places to promising students from the region. The Bush administration's Middle East Partnership Initiative, however – though its initial funding for FY2004 was only $29m – was slated for a ten-fold funding increase in the FY2005 budget request. Congressional follow-through would mean ample funding to expand universities' cultural-exchange capacities.

In addition to exchange programmes, the US must engage more actively with Arabic language media. Despite al-Jazeera's acutely anti-Western editorial bent right after 11 September, it has latterly become somewhat more even-handed. More generally, it has brought Islamic media into twenty-first century by expanding the access of Muslim populations to world news. The West, then, should view the rise of al-Jazeera as an opportunity to make its case to Islam for a new and better inter-cultural relationship. The hardest part of engaging with a broad public audience in the Arab and Muslim world will be substantive. The US will find it difficult to explain the US–Israeli relationship, the ongoing confrontation between Israel and the Palestinians, Washington's closeness to authoritarian regional governments and the serial abuses of Iraqi prisoners by their American (and to a lesser extent British) captors; to criticise Arab and Muslim societies and values; and to justify the effect of America's culture on the rest of the world. The paramount task will be for the US to make a more credible case that the war on terrorism is not a war on Islam, when bin Laden has used the normative terms of Islamic discourse to transform political grievances into violent Islamic imperatives.

The public-diplomacy issue raises the question of whether and how the US can engage indirectly in the religious debate within the Muslim world between 'fundamentalist' Salafists or Wahhabi-oriented clerics and more mainstream Muslims. The US itself would not be considered a legitimate interlocutor. But programmes for discreetly encouraging mainstream and orthodox clerics to rein in radical ones could start in the US itself. The American Muslim subculture is among the wealthiest and best assimilated in the West, and its extra-national cultural leadership should be nurtured and mobilised. Such programmes would also address the need to counteract American Muslims' new impulses towards radicalisation born of post-11 September suspiciousness on the part of the non-Muslim population.[25]

US coordination with European governments – especially France, Germany and Britain, which have more experience in engaging with Muslim populations – would be important to this effort. The intensive communication between the Indo–Pakistani Muslim diaspora and homeland communities suggests that government efforts to integrate them, and communicate through their newspapers and radio stations, might be the best way to reach an essentially hostile populace in Pakistan itself. Other diaspora could be approached in analogous fashion. Furthermore, Muslim intellectuals opposed to radical Islam should be accorded the same sanctuary that dissident Eastern European and Russian intellectuals received during the Cold War.[26]

Other fields of jihad

The threat from al-Qaeda and its affiliates is likely to grow in Central, South and Southeast Asia – the demographic, though not the spiritual, centre of Islam. Like the Gulf, Asia offers some full and reliable counter-terrorism partners. But like Saudi Arabia and Yemen, key regional states such as Pakistan and Indonesia remain affected by substantial militant forces. The Deobandi movement that produced the Taliban is the prime mover behind Islamic radicalisation in Pakistan. Although the influence of Wahhabi-influenced jihadists in Indonesia is less potent than that of the Deobandis on Pakistan, its ideological basis and social pathway through the madrassas and mosques is not dissimilar and should strike a cautionary chord. Such jihadists in Malaysia, the Philippines, and Singapore as well as Indonesia returned from Afghanistan after fighting the Soviets determined to unite the four countries into a single sharia-ruled caliphate – an objective consonant with bin Laden's transnational agenda.[27]

Transnational Islamic terrorist threats emanated from Malaysia, Singapore and the Philippines since well before 11 September. Although only Malaysia appears to have been alert to the early rumblings, the other two governments awakened quickly after the 11 September attacks. Their counter-terrorism cooperation with the West has since required little encouragement. The Pakistani and

Indonesian regimes are more problematic. They have secular vocations and wish to be regarded as effective coalition partners, but those regimes are also subject to significant popular and intra-governmental radical Islamic pressures that restrict their freedom of action. Thus, Islamabad's capacity to probe the 'tribal areas' primarily in Pakistan's Northwest Frontier Province in search of bin Laden has been limited, while it took the Bali bombing before Jakarta felt politically unfettered sufficiently to move against Jemaah Islamiah – and even since then has not done so decisively. The upshot is that there is a heavy premium on artful and eclectic Western diplomacy vis-à-vis these two capitals, which is required to improve intelligence and law-enforcement links. At the same time, owing to the resiliency of radical Islamist influences (particularly in Pakistan, where several attempts on Musharraf's life suggest appreciable Islamist penetration of the security forces) and their potential effect on regime survival, the West cannot expect seamless coordination.

Reviving military-to-military contacts and cooperation between the US and Indonesia, for example, could counter Islamist influences in the army and, by extension, government. Economic aid to Indonesia and Pakistan should be linked to the encouragement of moderate Islamic education – as indeed US assistance to Indonesia has been. Finally, conflict resolution could have a major impact – particularly in Kashmir, where easing tensions would take some of the steam out of radicalising elements in Pakistan and shrink al-Qaeda's regional recruitment pool. A policy emphasis on conflict resolution and honest mediation in the Middle East – which can be portrayed as highly respectful of sovereignty – could alter the perception among some Southeast Asian leaders that intervention in Iraq signals a new American imperialism that will impinge on the sovereignty of nations that the US deems hostile or problematic. More broadly, some of the local groups on which al-Qaeda increasingly relies for terrorist operations and certainly some diaspora remain chiefly concerned with local or regional problems. Effective conflict resolution or national political reconciliation could cause such groups and any expatriates associated with them to opt out of al-Qaeda's global jihad and its apocalyptic agenda.

Sub-Saharan Africa's basic counter-terrorism problem is more institutional than political. Most black African countries are not predominantly Muslim and, from Tanzania to Côte d'Ivoire, are wary of Islamic encroachment. While there do exist Muslim–Christian tensions in countries such as Tanzania and Côte d'Ivoire, they are often exaggerated for political effect by politicians seeking to elevate their country's relevance to the war on terror. At the same time, Nigeria's sectarian problems stand out as a potentially robust source of jihadist recruits and activity, and merit special attention. Countries like Kenya are plainly vulnerable to terrorist infiltration due to weak security forces preoccupied by violent tribal rivalries and perhaps seduced by historically peaceful Muslim minorities not perceived as serious threats. The proximity of East Africa to the Arabian Peninsula and to Somalia and Sudan – which have harboured substantial radical Islamic elements linked to al-Qaeda – and residual al-Qaeda infrastructure in Nairobi and Mombassa (never rolled up after the 1998 attacks on the US embassies) mean that the US and other major powers must continue strong preventive and deterrent measures, including aerial and maritime surveillance and ready special-forces deployments.[28] Poverty reduction and governmental reform constitute insurance against terrorist co-optation. Although Western nations have shown less attention than hoped to these areas immediately after 11 September, regional powers like South Africa and Nigeria have shown greater initiative in taking the fate of their continent in their own hands with the ambitious New Partnership for Africa's Development (NEPAD) and the establishment of the African Union.[29] In any case, serious improvement will take a number of years. In the meantime, outside actors may have to focus more sharply and expressly on strengthening counter-terrorism capabilities of – and not merely reforming – the security sector.[30]

Endgame?

Since the 11 September attacks, al-Qaeda has proven a resilient, pragmatic and elusive network of networks. It may take a generation to incapacitate al-Qaeda and its affiliates operationally. Whenever that might occur, a successor is likely to rise again unless the larger political environments that engendered al-Qaeda's emergence are decisively altered. To the extent that this involves diplomatic or economic efforts aimed at Muslim countries, the persuasion applied must be of the gentle variety. The US, for example, should be loath to jeopardise Egypt's peaceful disposition towards Israel or Saudi

Arabia's willingness to act as a 'swing producer' of oil by visiting excessive or impolitic diplomatic pressure on either state to liberalise and secularise too fast than domestic traditions and conditions will permit.[31]

Multilateral institutions are important for nurturing Western links, but their utility in providing political cover for essentially American agendas is limited. Borrowing nations, for instance, often see the IMF and the World Bank – which are important instruments of Western economic diplomacy – as tools of the United States and regard stringent debt conditionality as impinging on their sovereignty and imposing inequitable economic stresses. More broadly, bilateral donors should heed the lessons learned by the Bretton Woods institutions in the 1980s and 1990s. They often alienated developing nations by imposing too strictly the 'Washington Consensus' on neo-liberal economic reform (generally, market deregulation, privatisation of state-owned enterprises and trade liberalisation), and sometimes contributed to political instability by disrupting delicate economies that underpinned the 'performance legitimacy' of governments, as in Indonesia.[32] Similarly, military cooperation and assistance, such as that provided by the US to the Philippines and Yemen, can be effective, but have a limited counter-terrorism trajectory, and if excessive can also raise sensitivities about sovereignty and, worse, inspire rather than discourage grassroots anti-Western radicalisation. The Bush administration's idea of increasing foreign assistance to Muslim countries via the Millennium Challenge Account (MCA) is a step in the right direction in developing warmer relations with Islam, and harmonising Western and Islamic political, economic and cultural norms. But grants under the MCA should not be tethered too tightly to the Washington Consensus. A successful strategy would have to allocate funds to the dysfunctional governments as well as precocious ones.

Owing to the permeating and 'virtual' nature of al-Qaeda and the insusceptibility of its leaders to formal peace negotiation or settlement, victory in the 'war' on terror will not admit of clear identification. There will be no battlefield surrender and no signed armistice. Rather, victory is likely to reveal itself over time as a negative – the relative absence of terrorism – gradually confirmed by an increase in arrests and convictions and by more probative intelligence. Accordingly, there is no endgame as such to the campaign against transnational terrorism. There is only a pragmatic approach, inextricably involving both 'hard' counter-terrorism and 'transformative' counter-terrorism. These functions are non-optional and complementary. Hard counter-terrorism, along fairly clear operational parameters, is indispensable, and, in light of the difficulty of determining victory over terrorists, needs to be sustained even when a downturn in terrorist attacks leads to budgetary pressures on counter-terrorism resources. Transformative counter-terrorism, while essential for 'victory' and no less mandatory, will be highly contingent on emerging circumstances and subject to trial-and-error.

Chapter 4

Outperforming the Terrorists

In the three years following 11 September, the first priority was understandably and correctly self-protection via improved homeland security and enhanced law-enforcement and intelligence cooperation. Significant advances occurred over this period. Given the continued strength and appeal of al-Qaeda, and al-Qaeda's imperviousness to political co-optation, these remain indispensable. Greater efforts still are required to address the medium- and long-term challenges of eliminating the deeper causes of such terrorism. It is paramount that the US take the lead in this connection – not only because it possesses the most abundant resources but also because it is al-Qaeda's prime enemy. The more capable of stopping terrorism and terrorists and undermining their support structure the US can convince al-Qaeda that it is, the better it will be able to outflank the group politically as well as tactically.

Intellectual infrastructure and agenda

One of the US government's institutional failures prior to 11 September was its inability to anticipate new threats. Too many officials committed the fallacy of equating the familiar with the probable, and thus ignored the possibility of using civilian aircraft, in effect, as cruise-missiles.[1] Among the most important intellectual imperatives of the war on terrorism, then, is that of 'thinking outside the box' – or, as Dennis Gormley has put it, 'institutionalising imaginativeness' and 'enriching expectations'.[2] With the Manhattan Project, the government accomplished precisely that for offensive purposes, marshalling resources over a multi-year period in conditions of secrecy and urgency.[3] Indeed, that endeavour set the tone for the successful bureaucratisation of 'thinking about the unthinkable' during the Cold War, when the government overhauled the strategic force structure (including the nuclear navy) and built a national space-based reconnaissance system, among other things. These efforts refined the theory and practice of nuclear deterrence and enabled strategic stability to be achieved.

Thus far, the operational mobilisation undertaken by the West – and in particular the United States – has been, with qualifications, impressive. The intellectual mobilisation, however, has been wanting. Current policy thinking on grand strategy for dealing with the global jihad cleaves towards two extreme positions, one morally and politically unpalatable and the other risky and destructive. The first, premised on the belief that it is too late to fine-tune the policies that have alienated Muslims, involves the capitulation of the United States to the implicit demands of bin Ladenism, whereby the US would abandon Israel, jettison its strategic relationships with Saudi Arabia and Egypt, and forsake its leverage and standing in the Arab world.[4] The second envisages a full-scale Western mobilisation against transnational Islamist terrorism – a total war on terror. Under this scenario, the West's intelligence, law-enforcement and military assets would be brought to bear against any actual or potential terrorist strongholds or supporters as Muslim governments bandwagoned operationally and politically behind a hegemonic America.[5] The former would amount to negotiating with terrorists, and indeed yielding them victory, the latter to furnishing bin Laden, at prohibitively high risk, with precisely the violent 'clash of civilizations' that is integral to his apocalyptic eschatology.

Both positions are admittedly caricatures of viewpoints that are not quite so unsubtle. But the larger point is that post-9/11 strategic thinking has not found a realist middle ground. Nowadays the working premise of strategy, whether capitulatory or confrontational, is that talking to Muslims is essentially futile – that they must be either appeased or dominated. Yet the West hardly seems so intellectually barren as to be left to such crude and unsatisfactory dispensations. The transatlantic pragmatism that successfully steered grand strategy through the Cold War ought to hold more nuanced answers – a 'third way' through which the United States can both honour its commitments and strike an accommodation with Islam sufficient to marginalise bin Laden and his followers. That is the core challenge of terrorism. But it entails understanding what the diverse array of Muslims believe, why they believe it and how they think about the world and their place in it. This has customarily been the province of Middle East studies. In the United States and elsewhere, a wide range of intellectual influences – including the Vietnam War, post-colonial studies, deconstructionism, Edward Said's 'orientalism' thesis and US policy on the Israeli–Palestinian conflict as well as US Iraq policy since 11 September – have so politicised and polarised that discipline as to render academic establishments practically incapable of channelling the efforts of its constituents into a cohesive intellectual mobilisation in the interest of national security.

Accordingly, the US government should consider consolidating and concentrating the analysis of threats and long-term counter-terrorism strategy into a single government-chartered and funded think-tank, perhaps modelled on the RAND Corporation of the 1950s and 1960s. The composition of a RAND-type outfit geared to the age of sacred terror would be different from the group that coalesced to manage the threat of nuclear war. The challenge of the 1950s catered to distinctly American intellectual biases: an orientation towards the future, an urge to dominate it through superior energy and focus, and faith in technological progress and the capacity of the capitalist system to produce it. These strong suits are surely assets in the campaign against terrorism. But the absence of a cohesive and hierarchical adversary state and the asymmetric aspect of terrorists' tactics make them a very different, and on balance a more complicated, foe than the Soviet Union. The Soviets' strategic mindset resembled that of the Americans insofar as both aimed for international ideological primacy. The Manichean nature of the conflict for both the US and the Soviet Union simulated a zero-sum game, in which there was ultimately room for only one system. And indeed, the leadership of al-Qaeda may more closely resemble the Soviet politburo than it might first appear: as a secular religion, Marxism-Leninism was probably as potent and as absolute as bin Laden's militant brand of Wahhabism. But the compulsion of preserving the state stabilised US–Soviet relations. Thus, during most of the Cold War, both sides were more or less satisfied with nuclear parity, and through mutual deterrence made nuclear weapons unlikely warfighting tools. By contrast, al-Qaeda's leadership appears to view them as prime tools of religious deliverance. Further, today's threat from a flat network of non-state actors is far more heterogeneous than the highly centralised, state-controlled Soviet threat.

A new think-tank would, then, be substantively quite different from the old version. While the rational choice theory that RAND used, developed and came to epitomise will have a role to play, historical methods of analysis will be more important in determining its intellectual cast. The premium on physicists like Herman Kahn and mathematical logicians like Albert Wohlstetter will be lower. Regional experts will be important. But the new think-tank's approach will also have to avoid the analytic hazard of artificially chopping up Islam into regions of greater or lesser concern – e.g., the Persian Gulf versus sub-Saharan Africa. This tendency is incongruous with the permeating and global nature of the current terrorist threat, and has led to the neglect of potentially significant threats emanating from countries like Nigeria. So there will be considerable demand for experts on Islam as a whole and for sociologists of religion. Development economists will have to be rallied to apply their knowledge to areas of the world – in particular, the Middle East, whose oil-based economies have hindered balanced development and stalled their broad integration into the world economic system. Political scientists will be needed to determine how to transform authoritarian regimes that have alienated Muslim populations and moved them to look to Osama bin Laden for leadership into more participatory systems.

Deterrence still matters
The central issue of deterrence will admit of less elegant solutions in this long struggle than it did during the Cold War. But if it is a messy problem, no worthy research cohort will be able to dismiss the possibility of deterrence even in the face of enemies who often seem undeterrable. To be sure, many of al-Qaeda's hardcore members and followers are willing to martyr themselves for religious ends, unwilling to bargain explicitly and therefore difficult to counter by softer means. Deterrence in the sense of prevention through threatened punishment would not work with such people: they are unimpressed by America's military and political might except to the extent that it motivates them to kill Americans. Furthermore, al-Qaeda's political impermeability and consequent presumed

undeterrability were galvanising assumptions immediately after 11 September, when the US and its partners had to re-orient hard security and self-protection to deal with a rising strategic threat. The US did not exclude deterrence from its counter-terrorism policy, but it also was not sufficiently confident in deterrence to count it as one of the three pillars of national policy. Instead, NSPD-17 noted anticipatorily that 'more diverse and less predictable threats ... require new methods of deterrence'. Yet subsequent commentary on 'our contemporary deterrent posture' – about 'strong declaratory policy', 'political tools', the threat of 'overwhelming force ... including ... resort to all of our options', effective law-enforcement and intelligence – did not specify any 'new methods' or novel thinking tailored to the new threat.[6] This statement of national policy did not indicate with any particularity how the terrorist 'irreconcilables' might be deterred. But as the scarcity of post-11 September attacks in North America and Europe has suggested that governments have provisionally got a grip on hard counter-terrorism, American analysts have started to consider in greater depth how to re-conceive deterrence to meet terrorist threats – particularly from weapons of mass destruction (WMD). This intellectual task involves probing al-Qaeda's religious psychology.

A number of analysts have raised thoughtful questions in this vein.[7] John Parachini has illuminated the gap between al-Qaeda's intentions and capabilities; its capacity to make do with conventional explosives to produce mass-casualties; how that option could dampen WMD ambitions without appreciably reducing the overall terrorist threat and capability; and the need to preserve finite counter-terrorism resources via risk-management to a greater extent than the US government may have been willing to concede. These are all points well taken, though he seems too sanguine in asserting that 'bin Laden's worldview does not depend on the use of unconventional weapons' and that 'attacks with explosives or crashing jetliners into buildings will suffice'.[8] There remains a natural linkage between WMD and (1) high political impact of threshold-crossing terrorism like the 11 September attacks, and (2) the eschatology of radical Islam. Other US analysts are less inclined to downplay these factors. In an August 2003 symposium, Gregory Treverton, a relative sceptic on al-Qaeda's prospective use of WMD, said ruefully that '9/11 was shocking but a repeat would be less so. So there may be an incentive for terrorists to look to the next level of "stun" value'.[9] In the same gathering, Parachini himself admitted that there was a possibility that al-Qaeda might nurse a nascent chemical, biological, radiological or nuclear (CBRN) capability towards greater sophistication in the interest of achieving maximum impact.[10] Alluding to eschatology, Brian Jenkins stated that, 'believing they have the mandate of God, terrorists subscribing to ideologies drawn from religion are less constrained by conventional morality or assessments of personal risk' – characteristics that would underwrite WMD use. But he added a key qualification that has been gaining currency in the US: 'al-Qaeda and its affiliates are not monolithic institutions; they are complex institutions depending on tolerance and support. Deterrence in its traditional form may not work very well against the committed core or the wild-eyed recruits of enterprises like al-Qaeda, but other parts of the system may be amenable to influence'.[11]

There may be useful distinctions to make even within the hardcore category. For example, some Muslim terrorists regard WMD as indispensable instruments of eschatology. Others, however, seem to see them merely as prime warfighting assets, useful in compensating for the conventional military disparity between Western militaries and terrorists with no state apparatus. Terrorists in the first group are liable to use WMD as soon as they have them, those in the second more inclined to weigh the political and tactical tradeoffs crossing that threshold would entail.[12] The latter can probably be deterred – at least from using WMD.

The larger point is that in spite of the religiously absolute imperatives laid down by al-Qaeda's leadership, the highly dispersed and pragmatic character of the transnational Islamic terrorist network means that terrorists' religious and political intensity and tactical mindsets are highly variable. Like more manageable 'old' terrorist groups, al-Qaeda too encompasses professional terrorists and wavering 'fellow travellers' as well as maniacal true believers. It would be an obvious mistake to cast them as impervious to political, social and tactical influence.[13] In their confessions and statements, for instance, captured members of Turkish Hizbullah placed immense importance on perceived divine approval for their actions. They assumed that their leaders were not so much giving them orders as transmitting divine commands, and apprehended the success of their operations as proof of divine approval. But several militants said that when their leader – a man named Huseyin Velioglu – was killed, the organisation's archives captured and its cell network rolled up, they 'realised' that God was not on their side after all. Velioglu's death functioned as deterrence by denial of political objectives.[14] It is possible that the killing of a highly charismatic individual like bin Laden would actually enhance his iconic power through martyrdom and increase recruitment to militant organisations. The demonstrable failure of violent Islam to achieve its stated goals over a certain period of time, however, would probably erode assumptions of divine approval. The Turkish Hizbullah prisoners suggest that for many, such a period would be relatively short. Violent Islam would not disappear. But a large number of potential or actual perpetrators of violence would simply conclude: 'God isn't supporting this'. There is a precedent in the life of Mohammed for initial setbacks (i.e., the exile to Medina), but in the end he triumphed. So, in the medium-term, from a theological perspective, al-Qaeda's leadership still needs to be able to demonstrate both the validity of their assumptions about the predation of the West and progress in opposing it to sustain the momentum of the global jihad.[15]

Fashioning a comprehensive counter-terrorism policy, then, will require experts on Islam to identify who falls into what category in terms of amenability to influence, and operational analysts in the mould of the great nuclear strategists of the 1950s and 1960s to formulate non-proliferation and deterrence strategies for handling different brands of terrorist. More broadly, Thomas C. Schelling's conviction that 'most conflict situations are essentially bargaining situations' is not irrelevant to counter-terrorism.[16] Although al-Qaeda's shura – unlike, say, the IRA Army Council – is not interested in sitting down at a table and expressly negotiating with its adversaries, it is worth investigating what combinations of hard and soft counter-terrorism measures might strike what in the Cold War context Schelling dubbed 'tacit bargains' or 'coordination games' between the counter-terrorism coalition and the terrorists.[17] Looking even farther out, Lawrence Freedman has contemplated a norms-based deterrence-by-denial strategy. It would be established by persuading not the jihadists but the rest of the international community, especially wider Islam, to accept principles and relationships that comprehensively reject terrorism. Freedman observes that 'all political groups, however apparently fanatical in their ideology, adjust to shifting power relationships and act with some thought to the consequences'. Thus, if the West and non-radical Islam can eventually find common ground on civil and political norms, Muslim terrorists could be deterred – indeed, defeated – by the adverse weight of Muslim opinion, backed only remotely by the threat of force.[18]

Envisioning a successful counter-terrorism effort

Both al-Qaeda's extreme religious motivations and its operational flexibility make the organisation relatively unsusceptible to deterrence. The short US response to this characteristic, quite understandably, has been to re-emphasise military pre-emption or prevention as an option (though perhaps not, as some European commentators have claimed, a policy).[19] Al-Qaeda's post-Afghanistan dispersal has made the network increasingly impervious to military measures as well. It has also impelled the group to cede substantial operational initiative and responsibility to local groups – many of which, unlike, say, Egyptian Islamic Jihad, have not been defeated at national level. Thus, al-Qaeda has the potential to augment its transnational agenda of infiltration and disruption with more focused and traditional insurgencies. This may be happening in Iraq. The upshot is daunting: the coalition must develop military capabilities for limited quick-response action against certain terrorist activities – such as the establishment of a training camp in Somalia or Yemen – and for counter-insurgency in Iraq and possibly other places; yet its primary focus must be on uncovering and neutralising embedded cells and networks in the urban locales to which terrorists have spread, and which are not suitable for military action.

British officials have usefully identified several 'campaigns' comprising an overall counter-terrorism strategy. First, there is intelligence, or less clinically, gathering information on and understanding terrorists. Western governments, particularly European ones, have considerable experience along these lines, but the 'new' terrorists raise new challenges insofar as they are configured in horizontal networks of individuals trained to avoid hierarchies rather than vertical organisations. The second campaign is that of protecting the state and its population – what Americans call homeland security. This effort embraces civil preparedness and defence, hardening infrastructure and 'iconic' targets against attack, border security and aviation security. Third comes resilience – that is, building capacity to recover from attacks in case they occur. Fourth, the coalition must at once pursue the terrorists, dismantle their networks and blunt their motivations. The five-year objective of the strategy is to reduce the risk from transnational terrorism such that members of the general population can go about their business freely and with confidence. The campaigns embrace various missions. To reduce the terrorist threat, prevention is required. This involves tackling root causes through 'soft' measures. Threat reduction also requires 'hard' intelligence and law-enforcement measures that fall under the general heading of pursuit, while reducing vulnerability is strictly a matter of 'hard' security missions – to wit, protection and preparation. These four missions have overlapping timelines; thus, they are not alternative but complementary. The 'soft' measures to reduce the terrorist threat will take years to bear fruit; in the meantime, 'hard' measures must constrain terrorist networks.

The methods used in these campaigns are similar to those used against 'old' terrorist groups, but with a new emphasis on inter-governmental cooperation in light of the flat, transnational character of the 'new' terrorist threat. The fruits of that emphasis include forward measures such as the CSI (foreign port cooperation with US officials on container inspection) and the PSI (multinational cooperation in maritime, ground and air interdiction of suspected WMD cargo) as well as cooperative financial surveillance. But these are matters of immediate self-protection. Coalition counter-terrorism partners have a long way to go on consolidating threat reductions. In particular, they need to fortify international legal regimes – particularly in the non-proliferation area with respect to small arms, cruise-missiles and UAVs as well as ballistic missiles and WMD – and rebuild the foundational bilateral and multilateral relationships that were badly damaged over the 2003 US-led military intervention in Iraq.

Even if these challenges are well met, there are some persistent limits on how horizontal the counter-terrorism network can become – at least in the current strategic environment. Human intelligence is more difficult to develop on account of cultural and ethnic differences and because religious fervour makes al-Qaeda or affiliated operatives less likely to betray their own kind. Penetrating jihadist groups would require extraordinarily skilled recruiters and agent handlers, extraordinarily dedicated and resilient individuals prepared to operate undercover for a considerable length of time, or, ideally, both. Many heavily Muslim-populated countries – in particular, Saudi Arabia, Pakistan and Indonesia – are also subject to internal pressures and sympathies that make them disinclined to cooperate with Western governments. While terrorist attacks in those locales momentarily focus minds, the domestic constraints of radical Islam probably mean that robust counter-terrorism postures will not be consistently maintained. This means that homeland security, the proactive pursuit of terrorists and inter-governmental cooperation on the part of most Muslim countries is unlikely to match that of North American and European governments for the foreseeable future. In turn, with terrorists thus freer to recruit and stage from some non-Western countries, those three elements of counter-terrorism in the West will have to remain as robust and well-resourced as they have been since 11 September. But success in this regard will do no more than maintain the status quo – and leave the strategic threat of transnational mass-casualty terrorism salient. Thus, a wholesale and concerted effort among coalition partners will be required to marginalise radical Islam.

Radical Islam, in turn, will be difficult to temper. Al-Qaeda's physical dispersal, its religious zeal, its organisational and operational flexibility – all of these factors contribute to its considerable staying power. Politically, al-Qaeda already has considerable regional traction in the Muslim world. In the Middle East/Gulf region, continued bloodletting in the Israeli–Palestinian conflict; the persistence of what bin Laden terms 'apostate regimes' in Saudi Arabia, Egypt, Jordan and elsewhere; and the US occupation of Iraq give radical Islamists both causes with which to fuel recruitment and targets for the recruits to hit. In Asia, their cognates are India's perceived repression of Muslims in Kashmir; the fusion of Deobandism and Wahhabism in Pakistan, Afghanistan and other areas of Central Asia, and the hybrid's consequent militant expansionism; the US military presence in Central Asia; and grassroots pan-Islamism in Indonesia. In sub-Saharan Africa, weak states and counter-terrorism institutions (notably, in Kenya) present potentially hijack-able host states, while poverty and Islam's ongoing southward encroachment and flammable Muslim–Christian tensions in Côte d'Ivoire, Ethiopia, Nigeria, Senegal, Sudan and Tanzania set the table for recruitment and staging. Even on the fringes of Europe, the lethal November 2003 attacks in Istanbul indicate that the transnational jihadist movement may see Turkey as newly vulnerable to radicalisation, now that a party with Islamist credentials controls the government.

Finding an exemplar

Even with a government of a more Islamist hue than is customary, Turkey and its model of secular Islam may still point the way to convergence between Islam and the West. It has been acutely observed, of course, that Turkey's brand of secularism is sui generis and inseparable from Kemalism's authoritarian creed, and that the stability of Turkey's secular state rests on a distinctly illiberal and dominant military. Accordingly, Turkey is most realistically viewed as an example of how Islam and the West can coexist rather than a model that can be exported in toto to other countries. Yet, more ambitiously, the advent in 2002 of a ruling party with an Islamist pedigree – while perhaps an inchoate opportunity for jihadists – might also support an Islam–West rapprochement. While the Justice and Development Party (JDP) may be considered 'closet Islamists', they also appear to appreciate the ideological limits that Kemalism places on political Islam in Turkey – and indeed, the practical limits that the Turkish General Staff imposes.[20]

The JDP has a distinctly European vocation – not least for economic reasons – which constitutes a major constraint on its radicalisation. Thus, the EU should encourage the JDP's European tilt by moving ahead on Turkey's bid to join the union. There are several reasons why Brussels has been reluctant to register much encouragement. One is the unresolved status of the Cyprus dispute, which remains a separate – and serious – conflict-resolution problem. Another key factor is that the authoritarian role of the military derogates the Copenhagen governance criteria of EU membership. Yet the realities of Islamic doctrine – and indeed, the cautionary example of Iran – may suggest that secular control of the use of force within a Muslim country may be a prerequisite of a more broadly liberal state. An EU epiphany along these lines would relax its application of the Copenhagen criteria to Turkey, and enable it to set a definite date for talks with Ankara on EU accession. That would send the message that secular Muslim countries, including those with unabashedly religious leaders, are viable partners of Western nations.

Insofar as greater promise of EU membership could also copper-fasten the JDP's religious self-restraint, it might facilitate an accommodation between a tempered form of Islamism and the secular paternalism of the Turkish military that constitutes a shorter leap from the dynamic now prevailing in other Muslim countries. This would make the Turkish model a rich and realistic basis for a range of Western initiatives: from hard counter-terrorism assistance to nation-building to economic diplomacy.

Still, there is some need for a reality check with respect to Turkey. Its strategic relationship with the US, though intact, has suffered notably since the Turkish parliament failed to authorise the deployment of US ground troops in Turkey prior to the invasion of Iraq. More generally, although how Islamist the JDP is remains open to debate, Turkey definitely is not becoming more secular. What has dampened the resonance of Turkey as an exemplar is not so much the JDP itself as the uncertain impact that the JDP's being in power will have on Islamist militancy in Turkey. There is little doubt that non-violent Islamist hardliners, including some members of the JDP, are currently waiting to see whether Prime Minister Recep Tayyip Erdogan will deliver a more Islamicised state. But it is more difficult to know whether the JDP is having the same sedative impact on violent Islamists that the last Islamist-led government did in 1996–97, because their organisational networks have been so thoroughly compromised by the security forces that they lack operational capability. Al-Qaeda itself undoubtedly regards the JDP as a lackey of the West, perhaps even apostate. Virtually all of the Islamist violence in Turkey since the JDP took power has had a transnational jihadist connection. If the link between indigenous and transnational Islamists becomes firmer, Turkey will be a less attractive model.

Models of more limited applicability include Indonesia and, somewhat improbably, Iran. While radical Islamists have a voice in Megawati's secular government, Islamic radicalism in Indonesia is still an essentially marginal phenomenon. Retired General Susilo Bambang Yudhoyono's resounding 61% victory over Megawati in the September 2004 presidential election portends stronger central control of the security forces and, if anything, further sidelining of radical Islam. Although there is a broad trend towards greater religious observance, the majority of Indonesia's Muslim population remains tolerant in their outlook and adhere to the socio-religious standards of Nahdlatul Ulama (NU) and Muhammadiyah – essentially moderate social movements which together claim more than 70 million followers. NU, in fact, verges on being pro-Western. Both groups seek to extend religious principles through broad-based social programmes and support for political parties, and oppose the imposition of sharia law. These groups remain the dominant components of Indonesian civil society and the key constituencies of any government. Notwithstanding the rising threat of JI's pan-Islamic radicalism, NU and Muhammadiyah are examples of the kinds of institutions that the West should quietly encourage and support.

Iran has been mentioned as a potential template for a more progressive form of Islam, provided the reformist movement could prevail over the conservative establishment. Unfortunately, the conservatives' manipulation of the February 2004 national parliamentary elections consolidated their power. As long as the conservative camp remains politically entrenched, it is not likely to jettison the Ayatollah Ruhollah Khomeini's idiosyncratic doctrine of 'vilayat-e faqih' – 'rule of the religious jurisprudent' – under which clerics must rule the country directly rather than through the intermediary of secular authority. Nevertheless, Iran's democratic vocation developed through radical religious protest, sanctioned by the community of religious scholars (ulama), against secular authoritarianism in the 1920s that was reprised in the 1970s, and that vocation has subsequently acquired a more moderate cast.[21] It is possible, if not likely, that 'the success of the conservatives' strategy contains the seeds of their own destruction' – that their anti-democratic machinations will give rise to a broader and angrier movement that will jump the boundaries of conventional politics and orderly government all the way to counter-revolution.[22] Given that the Iranian right is itself divided between ideologues (under Supreme Leader Ayatollah Ali Khamanei) and pragmatists (led by powerful former president Akbar Hashemi Rafsanjani), sharing mainly an opposition to democratic pluralism, the conservatives do appear vulnerable. Iran's dependency on oil (which accounts for over 85% of its hard currency), lack of global economic integration and endemic corruption and unemployment, coupled with its population's youthfulness (70% are under 30) and high rates of urbanisation (70%) and literacy (above 80%), indicate a very weak popular base for the conservatives. It is also significant that in the 2001 presidential elections, 70% of the Revolutionary Guards – the Iranian military elements introduced by the clerical regime after the 1979 revolution – voted for reformist President Mohammed Khatami.

Iran's recent history, then, illustrates that a constructive religious–secular dialectic can operate in Islamic states. Radical Islam was central to political liberalisation in Iran, but economic pressures and civil libertarianism have gotten purchase there and spurred a more secular liberalism. Yet the fact remains that Iran owes its republic and its political identity to Islam. Its most important lesson for the West, then, may be that Muslim countries are not likely to be susceptible to thoroughgoing secularisation.

A forward-looking programme

The formulaic answer to the challenge of al-Qaeda's latency is to starve it of recruits and ultimately render it unable to mount a strategic campaign. This objective would in theory be accomplished by ameliorating motivationally inflammatory conflicts, strengthening counter-terrorism institutions in politically compromised Islamic and other states that are governmentally weak or underfunded, rebuilding failed states and bolstering weak ones, and liberalising authoritarian regimes so as to content the rising numbers of young Muslim men. This aim fits into the broad strategy for winning the Cold War: containment, deterrence, outperformance and engagement.

If, three years after 11 September, the global counter-terrorism coalition had provisionally contained transnational Islamic terrorism, that was all it had done. It had yet to outperform the terrorists. The problematic US-led intervention in Iraq was a step backwards. Immediately following the Iraq intervention, al-Qaeda and linked groups sharpened their focus from soft targets of opportunity in scattered locales to the Arab world. The areas of greatest immediate interest were Iraq itself and Saudi Arabia, bin Laden's 'near enemy'. The fraught nature of the Iraq occupation extended the motivational boost that the occupation has given global as well as local terrorists, and simultaneously delayed any countervailing suppressive effects on terrorism that might spring from political reform in the region. Foreign jihadists were able to establish links with the indigenous insurgency in Iraq (where they had a toe-hold in the remnants of Ansar al-Islam and a ready liaison in Abu Musab al-Zarqawi), build up terrorist infrastructure in Saudi Arabia and follow through on an intensifying inclination to target close US partners and allies, starting with Saudi Arabia, moving on to Morocco, Saudi Arabia again, Turkey and finally Spain over the course of ten months. Then local al-Qaeda talent in Saudi Arabia stepped up attacks on foreign oil personnel – a target choice of potential economic as well as political import, and one designed to avoid the collateral damage of Saudi casualties which in the 2003 attacks probably cost al-Qaeda popular Arab support. At the same time, intelligence 'chatter' pointed to the likelihood of a major attack on US soil in 2004. Jemaah Islamiah – probably the most effective of al-Qaeda's affiliates – and linked groups in the Philippines remained active in Southeast Asia.

The post-Afghanistan, post-Iraq transnational Islamist terrorist network, though more dispersed and less tightly controlled by the leadership of al-Qaeda itself, is not in retreat. To the contrary, since the Iraq intervention it has appeared increasingly to be on the offensive. The intervention increased the global terrorist network's recruiting power by lending credence – at least from the standpoint of the many Muslims already suspicious of the West – to bin Laden's claims, in effect, that the US seeks to perpetuate the humiliation of Islam by increasing its military, political and economic influence in the Muslim world. America's preoccupation with problems in Iraq has also caused Washington to pay less attention to the Israeli–Palestinian conflict than it would have otherwise. That conflict – though not a passionate concern for bin Laden himself – genuinely upsets many Muslims worldwide and its continuation bolsters al-Qaeda's ability to enlist new followers. But perhaps the highest cost that the Iraq adventure has imposed on the war on terror has been that of increasing the political toxicity of America in Islamic countries.

To outperform al-Qaeda et al., the West needs to effect a political convergence between itself and Islam. Steven Simon has nicely articulated the general prescription:

> *The United States and its partners … need to persuade Muslim populations that they can prosper without either destroying the West or abandoning their traditions to the depredations of Western culture. That is a long-term project. American and allied determination in war against apocalyptic*

– and therefore genocidal – religious fanatics must be coupled with a generosity of vision about postwar possibilities. Islam's warm embrace of the West is too stark a reversal to expect in the foreseeable future. However, it is feasible to lay the foundation for a lasting accommodation by deploying the considerable economic and political advantages of the United States and its allies.[23]

Serious Western political engagement in the resolution of conflicts that anger Muslims is one important way to demonstrate a 'generosity of vision'. In practice, of course, conflicts are difficult to tame, and vulnerable states difficult to repair. At least in the short term, liberalisation and security institution-building often work at cross-purposes: authoritarian regimes are generally best at hard counter-terrorism, but this ultimately tends to export and transnationalise terrorism. There are scarce resources for the state-building required to regenerate failed and weak states, further strained by the overwhelming state-building and counter-insurgency tasks yet to be completed in Iraq and Afghanistan. This is not to say that medium-term progress in these areas will be impossible. The US commitment to de-escalating violence in the Middle East is durable if variable, and there may be greater scope emerging for facilitating an accommodation between India and Pakistan on Kashmir. Security-sector reform involving both high-performance and good-governance incentives could start to reconcile counter-terrorism and political reform.[24]

Familiar technocratic prescriptions for exerting a positive influence on Islam include the political reform of authoritarian, non-participatory regimes in Arab and other Muslim countries that have alienated and radicalised their youth; a more thorough economic integration of the economies of those countries into the global system; and promotion of Muslim women's rights and general literacy levels to, among other things, slow the burgeoning population growth that will otherwise produce ever younger and more flammable Muslim societies. These require better public diplomacy on the part of the West and more foreign development assistance. But the key challenge now, in the post-Iraq world, is how to ensure that the processes of effecting moderating changes in the Islamic world avoid offending the very Muslims the West seeks to win over.

In this area, policymakers need to understand that both nationalism and jihadism operate among militant Muslims and that – given the partial infiltration of the indigenous Iraqi insurgency by jihadists – are not necessarily mutually exclusive. Nationalism is now subordinate to global jihadism as a force in political Islam, but it certainly is not dead. Beyond Iraq, for example, a form of nationalism, albeit underpinned by religion, animates militancy among Pakistani and Kashmiri Muslims more than global jihadism does. This reinforces the view that the governments of Muslim countries, problematic as they may be, need to be treated with caution and ostensible respect in advancing Western diplomatic, political and economic initiatives in the Muslim world. If there were ever a possibility that the US could bypass illiberal regimes and directly engage with Muslim populations – a dubious proposition in any event – Iraq has foreclosed it. American economic and political initiatives will now have to be laundered through existing state apparatuses. This more gradual approach is not a bad thing, however, as it will tend to minimise the risk, among others, that anti-Western regimes would succeed existing ones as liberalisation proceeds. Frustrating as it may be, the House of Saud is far preferable to a bin Ladenist theocracy as an interlocutor for western democracies. This reality dictates that, while the West cannot default to the status quo in the Greater Middle East, it has little choice but to remain risk-averse.

There are limits to the potential for liberalising Islam. They appear constraining but not unavailing. It is true that under Muslim religious doctrine there is little room for a meaningful separation of church and state: the state theoretically has no sovereignty, which rests with God and the sharia. Furthermore, owing to that and the sanctity of established clerics' interpretation of the Koran, there is little chance of a secular Reformation. Yet in Islam's own realpolitik, laws and secular institutions have proven necessary – however paradoxically – to maintain the primacy of religious institutions.[25] It is worth noting that Iran and Saudi Arabia are the only true Islamic republics – that is, states in which supreme constitutional power resides in the ulama. In Iran, a reformist movement has made significant inroads against the conservative religious establishment – primarily via the machinery of democracy. Saudi Arabia has not witnessed the same evolution so far, but may become more susceptible to it with limited democratic reforms that Riyadh has seen fit to introduce following the US military withdrawal from the country facilitated by the ouster of Saddam Hussein's regime. The unfolding of reform in Iran and smaller Gulf Cooperation Council states such as Bahrain and Qatar has led one Muslim scholar to suggest that 'it is precisely democracy – a democracy derived from, and not in spite of, Islamic principles – that offers the most viable route to rapprochement between Islam and the west'.[26] In that light, American political assumptions about transforming Iraq were only about half right: democracy was the remedy for moving Iraq and the region forward, but it could not be rendered by a coercive military intervention.

Muslim states are more susceptible than others to risks of political and cultural alienation and insularity precisely because of the inherent irreconcilability of Islamic doctrine and secular liberalism.[27] In searching for common ground, Western powers need to better appreciate doctrinal distinctions within Islam. In particular, they should acquire a more refined understanding of the difference between orthodox and radical Islam. Although elements of the former may well be anti-Western, they also interpret the dictates of jihad far more narrowly than radicals and tend to oppose violence; thus, the orthodox should be regarded as at least potential, though limited, counter-terrorism partners. While moderate Muslims could be more robust partners, scope for mobilising them against radicals remains circumscribed by the very fact that moderates are by definition averse to confrontation and fearful of being branded impious or, worse, apostate.[28] These considerations suggest that Western powers stand the best chance of winning over non-radical Muslims by centring their political effort on the values that are least controversial in both the Christian and the Muslim world. These will tend to involve human rights (especially religious tolerance, running in both directions) rather than systemic political ideals like pristine elections. Western diplomacy should also avoid any suggestion that Western secularism or indeed Christianity abhors Muslim piety, and that the two cannot coexist. Otherwise, the sense of historical geopolitical humiliation that some Muslims share with bin Laden will only be amplified and expanded.[29] Like caveats apply to unrestrained infiltration of Western products and media into Muslim commerce: selective and measured globalisation may be part of the answer, but rampant and insensitive globalisation is assuredly part of the problem.

Finally, if the US and its partners had best nurture incrementalism rather than revolution with respect to Islam's acclimation to Western values, they should also fully recognise and uphold those values in making their case to the Muslim world. The political impact of the Abu Ghraib revelations was greater than the collateral damage that any errant coalition bomb could cause. Avoiding future political disasters means carefully circumscribing conditions for the use of force (including its pre-emptive or preventive use); using international law and diplomacy to attain strategic objectives where possible; and ensuring that civil liberties are protected even though the ubiquity of terrorist threats will require more intrusive and prophylactic security. In addition, the new security environment may call for modifications to international legal norms governing sovereignty, intervention and armed conflict. But in arriving at these changes, the US and its partners should honour the rule of law by publicly broaching and establishing new legal standards in public forums through debate and consensus – something that did not immediately happen with respect to the battlefield detainees held in Guantanamo Bay, for example. In the absence of transparency and evenhandedness on the West's part in applying its own principles, Muslim governments and populations are unlikely to be convinced of either the West's good faith towards Islam or its intramural integrity.

Notes

Acknowledgments

The author would like to thank Sir David Omand GCB, KCB, Security and Intelligence Co-ordinator and Permanent Secretary, UK Cabinet Office, for his invaluable comments on an earlier draft of this paper; Steven Simon, Senior Analyst at the RAND Corporation, for his ongoing insights and advice; Gareth Jenkins, IISS Consulting Senior Fellow, for his perceptive comments on political Islam and Turkish political trends; and James Hackett, IISS Research Analyst, for his thorough review of an earlier draft. Any mistakes, of course, are the author's sole responsibility.

Introduction

[1] Paul R. Pillar, *Terrorism and U.S. Foreign Policy* (Washington DC: Brookings Institution Press, 2001), pp. 50–56

[2] Ibid, p. 29.

[3] 'Terrorism' is a method of violent coercion usefully defined as the premeditated, politically motivated targeting of or threat against non-military or non-combatant persons or facilities by non-state actors, usually by asymmetric means, in order to intimidate civilian populations or some other audience extending beyond the direct targets and thereby produce changes in the policy of a government or governments. See generally Pillar, *Terrorism and U.S. Foreign Policy*, pp. 12–18. Terrorist acts can also have subsidiary purposes, such as recruitment. Many, if not most, armed non-state groups have attributes of both terrorists and paramilitary insurgencies. For example, the Provisional Irish Republican Army, the Liberation Tigers of Tamil Eelam, the Lebanese group Hizbullah and the Palestinian armed groups have targeted both military and non-military personnel and assets.

[4] See, e.g., Jonathan Stevenson, 'Irreversible Peace in Northern Ireland?', *Survival*, vol. 42, no. 3, Autumn 2000, pp. 5–26.

[5] See Daniel Benjamin and Steven Simon, 'Pan Am 103: Keep Up the Fight', *Washington Post*, 1 February 2001, p. A21.

[6] See Steven Simon and Daniel Benjamin, 'America and the New Terrorism', *Survival*, vol. 42, no. 1, spring 2000, pp. 59–75; 'The Terror', *Survival*, vol. 43, no. 4, winter 2001, pp. 5–17.

[7] This distinction was developed by Glenn H. Snyder, *Deterence and Defence: Toward a Theory of National Security*, (Princeton, NJ:

Princeton University Press, 1961), pp. 14–16

8 Quoted in, for example, David Johnston and David Rohde, 'Terrorism Suspect Taken to US Base for Interrogation', *New York Times*, 17 September 2002, p. A1.

9 See Jonathan Stevenson, 'Pragmatic Counter-terrorism', *Survival*, vol. 43, no. 4, winter 2001, pp. 35–48.

10 See, e.g., IISS, 'Al-Qaeda: One Year On', *Strategic Comments*, vol. 8, issue 7, September 2002.

11 Ibid.

12 Quoted in Michael Elliott, 'Reeling Them In', *Time*, 23 September 2002, p. 30.

Chapter 1

1 See generally Daniel Benjamin and Steven Simon, *The Age of Sacred Terror* (New York: Random House, 2002), chapters 7 and 8.

2 Ibid., pp. 340–48. See generally *The 9/11 Commisson Report: Final Report of the National Commission on Terrorist Attacks Upon the United States* (New York: W. W. Norton & Co., 2004)

3 Raymond Bonner and Jane Perlez, 'Bali Bomb Plotters Said to Plan to Hit Foreign Schools in Jakarta', *New York Times*, 18 November 2002, p. 1. Besides Europe and Southeast Asia, established fields of jihad include Egypt, Saudi Arabia, Jordan, Palestine, Algeria, Pakistan and Central Asia. See Benjamin and Simon, *The Age of Sacred Terror*, chapter 5.

4 See Notice, Office of the Attorney General; Homeland Security Advisory System, Federal Register 12047, 18 March 2002. For fear of causing panic or inducing scepticism by 'crying wolf', however, the US government has been circumspect about issuing official national public alerts, though more liberal in apprising state and local authori-

ties of threats.

5 Neil A. Lewis and Don Van Natta Jr., 'Ashcroft Offers Accounting of 641 Charged or Held', *New York Times*, 28 November 2001, p. A1.

6 See John J. Miller, 'A Junior al Qaeda', *National Review*, 31 December 2001.

7 David E. Kaplan, 'Made in the U.S.A.', *US News & World Report*, 10 June 2002. Indeed, one of the alleged al-Qaeda cell members arrested in Lackawanna, New York in September 2002 admitted to going to Afghanistan for religious training. All nine of those arrested as suspected members of the Lackawanna cell were US citizens of Yemeni origin.

8 See Daniel Benjamin and Steven Simon, 'The Worst Defense', *New York Times*, 20 February 2003.

9 The countries given priority on the basis of their respective numbers of visa applicants were Egypt, Indonesia, Morocco, Pakistan and the United Arab Emirates. The DHS planned to open offices in these countries in early 2004. See Philip Shenon, 'Homeland Security Dept. Planning 7 Offices Overseas to Screen Visas', *New York Times*, 7 October 2003.

10 Susan Sachs, 'U.S. Crackdown Sets Off Unusual Rush to Canada', *New York Times*, 25 February 2003. Under a new registration programme that began in December 2002, of 32,000 foreign men registered by mid-February 2003, 3,000 faced deportation.

11 See Clifford Krauss, 'In Antiterror Effort, Canada's Authorities Use Surveillance More Than Arrests', *New York Times*, 13 March 2003.

12 Immediately after 11 September, the US Customs Service was capable of inspecting only 2% of the containers coming into the United States. Although forward port screening under the CSI has substantially reduced risks, as of

August 2004 only about 4% of the containers entering the US were being inspected. The inspection regime does need to become tighter. But approaching anything like a 100% inspection rate would be impracticable. The primary objective is to establish common standards for physical security, reporting and information-sharing for operators, conveyances and cargo, and a multilateral system for enforcing compliance with those standards. Particular measures include: requiring containers to be loaded in electronically monitored, security-sanitised facilities; affixing global-positioning system transponders and electronic tags to trucks and containers to facilitate tracking; installing theft- and tamper-resistant seals on containers; mandating background checks for personnel processing cargo or vehicles; instituting the use of biometric travel identity cards; and establishing inter-agency data links from point of departure to point of entry. The logical multilateral body for coordinating and implementing forward homeland security measures is the International Maritime Organisation (IMO). At a 9–13 December 2002 conference, the IMO established the International Ship and Port Security Code, which took effect in July 2004. The code exhorts IMO members to facilitate the long-range technical identification and tracking of ships and the maintenance of continuous onboard itinerary records and to conduct comprehensive risk assessments at port facilities. But the Code stops short of supporting US proposals for background checks which must first be approved by the International Labour Organisation. Contrary to American preferences, the Code also does not require biometric identification devices for seafar-

ers, and international sharing of information on the ultimate ownership of vessels.

13 See Jerry Seper, 'Al-Qaeda Seeks Tie to Local Gangs', *Washington Times*, September 2004, p. 41

14 The Multistate Anti-Terrorism Information Exchange (MATRIX) employs computer software to comb through records kept by state and federal agencies compiled in a single database to yield a list of people statistically likely to be terrorists. An early iteration of the system produced 120,000 names. Because MATRIX's database includes records on innocent people as well as known criminals, and appears to be relatively indiscriminating, civil libertarians oppose its use and only five states remain active in the programme.

15 In at least one case before 11 September, the FAA approved the use of a UAV for potential agricultural applications provided that the vehicle's wingspan not exceed 2.9 metres, that it be called a 'model airplane' rather than a UAV, and that it be flown below 3,000 metres. Restrictions of this sort may be convenient from an air safety standpoint. But such 'model airplanes', however limited their payload capacity (probably 11–23kg), can still be readily equipped to deliver a sufficient quantity of biological agent to produce devastating effects. Indeed, a model aircraft's very small size that conveniently permits it to fit into the largest Federal Express package for shipment anywhere around the globe. Dennis Gormley has done much of the groundbreaking work in analysing the potential dangers from cruise-missiles and UAVs. See, e.g., Dennis M. Gormley, *Dealing With the Threat of Cruise Missiles*, Adelphi Paper 339 (Oxford: Oxford University Press for the IISS, 2001).

[16] See Benjamin and Simon, 'The Worst Defense'.

[17] See Richard A. Clarke, *Against All Enemies: Inside America's War on Terror* (New York: The Free Press, 2004)

[18] See generally, Stephen E. Flynn, *America the Vulnerable: How Our Government is Failing to Protect Us From Terrorism* (New York: HarperCollins, 2004).

[19] Planning materials seized in the Europe-wide raids in December 2002 and January 2003 indicated that NATO bases and the London underground could be targets. See 'Tackling a Hydra', *The Economist*, 30 January 2003.

[20] See, e.g., S. Gorka, 'Al-Qaeda: The Link and Threat to Europe', *Jane's Terrorism & Security Monitor*, 1 January 2003.

[21] See Jonathan Stevenson, 'How Europe and America Defend Themselves', *Foreign Affairs*, vol. 82, no. 2, March/April 2003, pp. 76–77. Among the European countries that have faced serious terrorism problems on their own soil – France, Germany, Italy, Spain and the UK – only France ever lent credence to the sanctuary doctrine, and certainly no longer does so. See Jeremy Shapiro and Bénédicte Suzan, 'The French Experience of Counter-terrorism', *Survival*, vol. 45, no. 1, spring 2003, pp. 67–97. But Belgium, which has never experienced terrorism at home, has applied the doctrine and has a problematically bifurcated security system that makes it highly vulnerable to terrorist infiltration. See Christopher Bouchek, 'Special Report – Belgium: The Epicentre of Terrorism in Europe', *Jane's Terrorism & Security Monitor*, 1 March 2003. The assessment indicated by the title of this article appears to be an exaggeration.

[22] See, e.g., Bouchek, 'Special Report – Belgium: The Epicentre of Terrorism in Europe'.

[23] See, e.g., Charles M. Sennott, 'Wide Dragnet Splinters al-Qaeda', *Boston Globe*, 21 June 2002, p. A20.

[24] See, for instance, Jim Hoagland, 'A New Disconnect with Europe', *Washington Post*, 14 April 2002, p. B7.

[25] See, e.g., Susan Bell, 'Britain in Row With France as Bomb Terrorism Trial Opens', *The Scotsman*, 2 October 2002, p. 13.

[26] Karl Cushing, 'Security Concerns at Immigration Database Launch', *Computer Weekly*, 23 January 2003, p. 14; Rachel Fielding, 'System Will Simplify Asylum Process', *Computing*, 30 January 2003, p. 20.

[27] Some European civil-liberties activists found even this safeguard unsatisfactory. See, e.g., 'Asylum-seekers Set to Face Fingerprint Rule Across EU', *EIU ViewsWire*, 17 January 2003.

[28] Theoretically, NATO structures could be useful in coordinating homeland-security efforts. As of June 2002, the alliance had undertaken five concrete counter-terrorism initiatives. With the exception of a deployable nuclear, biological and chemical analytical laboratory, these consisted mainly of marshalling first-response capabilities and joining up experts via web resources. NATO's civilian budget remains small. Between its impending enlargement and the need to reconsider its mission, NATO cannot be expected to apply itself swiftly and diligently to counter-terrorism problems. In mid-2003, the Atlantic Council of the United States established an impressive panel of experts, co-chaired by former US National Coordinator for Security Infrastructure and Counterterrorism Richard A. Clarke and General Barry McCaffrey, to explore an appropriate international counter-terrorism role for NATO. In its project summary, the Atlantic Council noted

that counter-terrorism 'is a new mission area for NATO. To undertake it fully will require building new doctrine, strategies and well-integrated multinational training at a time when achieving consensus to implement the necessary measures may be increasingly difficult. It may also require new commitments of national force capabilities and a new approach to civil-military relations'.

29 The tendency in Europe seems to be for private industry to look to government for help in managing the risks of terrorism, rather than vice-versa. Commenting on the formation of a new insurer to underwrite terrorism insurance, one European insurance executive said: 'In this huge new situation, industry cannot cover everything alone. There has to be some government role. The potential losses are incalculable. But this shows that private industry can do something'. 'Insurers Create European Terrorism Underwriter', *Best's Insurance News*, 4 April 2002.

30 In Germany, for example, as of August 2002 only 212 of about 4,000 companies agreed to hand over personnel records that the government sought to check against profiles of the 11 September hijackers. See Ian Johnson and David Crawford, 'Corporate Defiance: Germany's Hunt for Terrorists Hits Unlikely Obstacle', *Wall Street Journal*, 9 August 2002, p. A1.

31 Daniel Dombey, 'EU Deal Agreed on Internet Privacy', *Financial Times*, 31 May 2002, p. 6.

32 See Kristin Archick, 'Europe and Counterterrorism: Strengthening Police and Judicial Cooperation', Report for Congress, Congressional Research Service (Washington DC: Library of Congress, 23 July 2002), pp. 13–14; Raf Casert, 'Ashcroft, EU Counterparts Seek Closer

Cooperation in Battle Against Terrorism', *Associated Press*, 11 September 2002.

33 See Craig S. Smith 'Few Nations check to see if passports are stolen, Interpol says', *New York Times*, 23 August 2004.

34 CIA, 'Terrorist CBRN: Materials and Effects (U),' CTC 2003-40058, May 2003; National Infrastructure Protection Center, 'Homeland Security Information Update: Al Qa'ida Chemical, Biological, Radiological, and Nuclear Threat and Basic Countermeasures', *Information Bulletin* 03-003, 12 February 2003.

35 Since the removal of Saddam Hussein from power in Iraq, it has become clearer that al-Qaeda had no operational connections to his regime, and that the regime in any case probably had no usable WMD to offer al-Qaeda at the time of the 2003 intervention.

36 The general concern is registered in Director of Central Intelligence, 'Unclassified Report to Congress on the Acquisition of Technology Relating to Weapons of Mass Destruction', 1 January through 30 June 2003 (submitted November 2003).

37 'National Strategy to Combat Weapons of Mass Destruction', *National Security Presidential Directive* 17, 17 September 2002 (unclassified version released December 2002).

38 Some Americans, of course, disagree. E.g., Robert Kagan, 'America's Crisis of Legitimacy', *Foreign Affairs*, vol. 83, no. 2, March/April 2004, p. 69.

39 Some prominent European commentators recognised a need for European governments to take the threat more seriously after 11 September; e.g., Thérèse Delpech, *International Terrorism and Europe*, Chaillot Paper no. 56, Institute for Security Studies, December 2002, p. 31. See also 'Non-proliferation in the 21st Century: A

Transatlantic Agenda', Draft General Report, NATO Parliamentary Assembly, 22 September 2003. Other European analysts, however, have seemed self-consciously unalarmed. See, for example, Harald Müller, *Terrorism, Proliferation: A European Threat Assessment*, Chaillot Paper no. 58, Institute for Security Studies, March 2003, pp. 70–72.

[40] Aimed at a population inured to IRA terrorism, such pronouncements are designed to promote public awareness of terrorist threats and thus increase security. But some have suggested that they also underrate the potential preventive capabilities of re-oriented counter-terrorism regimes and perversely confirm the terrorists' capacity to influence behaviour and thus may embolden them. See Crispin Black, 'Never Say Inevitable', *Guardian*, 7 April 2004.

[41] Although the UK's civil-defence budget has increased by 35% over pre-2001 levels, it is still only £35m per annum and faces a considerable challenge in rebuilding a system that was dismantled in 1991–92 after the Cold War ended. Even when it was intact, with a system of regional headquarters, the system's response time was measured in days. It would be difficult, perhaps impossible, to deploy comprehensive preventive means to compensate for any first-response deficiencies.

[42] See Ken Menkhaus, *Somalia: State Collapse and the Threat of Terrorism*, Adelphi Paper 364 (Oxford: Oxford University Press for the IISS, 2004), pp. 70–71.

[43] Ibid., pp. 71–75.

[44] For example, Susan Rice – until 2000 Assistant Secretary of State for African Affairs – testified to House Subcommittee on Africa that it was 'imperative' that the US 'invest tens of millions of dollars annually in helping build counter-crime and counter-terrorism capacity in a number of African countries', to 'pay the price, billions and billions, to lift the peoples of Africa ... out of hopelessness and poverty'. She then pointed out that Africa's share of the first post-11 September US Foreign Operations budget would be smaller than that of the previous year. Prepared Statement of Susan E. Rice, 'Africa and the War on Global Terrorism', Hearing Before the Subcommittee on Africa of the Committee on International Relations, House of Representatives, 107th Congress, First Session, 15 November 2001, Serial No. 10746, pp. 15–17.

Chapter 2

[1] Jane Perlez, 'Key Suspect in Bali Bombing is Said to Confess', *New York Times*, 22 November 2002, p. A1.

[2] See David Johnston, 'U.S. Agency Sees Global Network for Bomb Making', *New York Times*, 22 February 2004.

[3] Benjamin and Simon, *The Age of Sacred Terror*, p. 215.

[4] See generally IISS, 'Al-Qaeda Targets Europe', *Strategic Comments*, vol. 10, issue 2, March 2004.

[5] See Shapiro and Suzan, 'The French Experience of Counter-terrorism', pp. 69–80.

[6] The seminal article on this distinction is Steven Simon and Daniel Benjamin, 'America and the New Terrorism,' *Survival*, vol. 42, no. 1, spring 2000, pp. 59–75. In 1999, 30.5% of MI5's £140m budget was devoted to the Northern Irish terrorist threat, compared to 22.5% to international terrorist threats. British analysts have concluded that the United Kingdom's security services neglected the threat from al-Qaeda due to their preoccupation with

Northern Irish terrorism. E.g.,
Fraser Nelson, 'MI5 Accused of
Ignoring al-Qaeda', *Scotsman*, 20
June 2002, p. 20. Similarly,
German counter-terrorism
authorities were focused on neo-
Nazi, rather than Islamic, threats.
Douglas Frantz and Desmond
Butler, 'The 9/11 Inquest: Did
Germans Bungle?', *New York
Times*, 11 July 2002, p. A1.

7 For a pre-11 September view on
this difference, see Bruce
Hoffman, 'Is Europe Soft on
Terrorism?,' *Foreign Policy*, no.
115, summer 1999, pp. 62–76.

8 Erik van der Linde, et al., 'Quick
Scan of Post-9/11 National
Counter-terrorism Policymaking
and Implementation in Selected
European Countries', Research
Project for the Netherlands
Ministry of Justice, RAND
Europe, May 2002, pp. 6, 27–29.

9 These details were given in a talk
entitled 'Al-Qaeda's European
Front: 9/11 and its Implications',
by Fernando Reinaros, Professor
of Political Science at King Juan
Carlos University and Senior
Adviser to Spain's Minister of the
Interior at the Woodrow Wilson
International Center for Scholars,
in Washington, DC on 27
September 2004.

10 Archick, 'Europe and
Counterterrorism: Strengthening
Police and Judicial Cooperation',
pp. 2–5.

11 See 'Tackling a Hydra', *Economist*,
30 January 2003.

12 Observed one journalist: 'The EU
members states say it is not worth
sharing information with Europol
because it is ineffective; Europol
says it is ineffective because it is
not given information'. Judy
Dempsey, 'Europol Labours to
Forge Bonds Among EU's
Crimefighters', *Financial Times*,
28 February 2002. See also Axel
Krause, 'Europol: A European
FBI?', *Europe*, February 2002,
p. S1.

13 In February 2002, Eurojust, a
complement of prosecutors and
magistrates, was activated to
coordinate joint investigations
and the prosecution of serious
cross-border crimes.

14 Archick, 'Europe and
Counterterrorism: Strengthening
Police and Judicial Cooperation',
p. 6.

15 See, for example, Gordon Corera,
'How Militant Islam Found a
Home in London', *Jane's
Intelligence Review*, August 2002,
pp. 15–19.

16 See Zahid H Bukari,
'Demography, Identity, Space:
Defining American Muslims', in
Philippa Strum and Danielle
Tarantolo, *Muslims in the United
States: Demography, Beliefs,
Institutions* (Washington DC:
Woodrow Wilson International
Center for Scholars, 2003), pp. 7–8.

17 See Josh Meyer, Eric Lichtblau
and Bob Drogin, 'Gains and Gaps
in Sept. 11 Inquiry', *Los Angeles
Times*, 10 March 2002, p. A1.

18 Where legal process is not readily or reliably available, European
objections to extra-judicial
American measures have been
muted. For instance, European
officials and media raised few
serious objections when the CIA
used a Predator UAV armed
with Hellfire antitank missiles to
kill six al-Qaeda members in
Yemen in November 2002. There
was at least a tacit recognition
that neutralising them via law-
enforcement – particularly in
countries, like Yemen, where
state institutions were weak or
politically compromised – would
not always be possible. The fact
that the Yemeni government had
consented to the operation also
moderated reactions to the inci-
dent.

19 See 'US Domestic Intelligence
Initiatives', IISS, *Strategic
Comments*, vol. 9, issue 1, January
2003.

20 Although TTIC is not generally viewed as being optimally effective, intelligence reform in general and integration in particular became a Congressional and White House priority in late 2004.

21 See Dana Priest and Douglas Farah, 'Terror Alliance Has U.S. Worried', *Washington Post*, 30 June 2002, p. A1.

22 See Stevenson, 'How Europe and America Defend Themselves', pp. 76, 85.

23 See Marc Champion, 'On Issues of Security, U.S. Needs Lessons', *Wall Street Journal Europe*, 12 June 2002, p. A2. See also Hoffman, 'Is Europe Soft on Terrorism?', pp. 73–75.

24 See James Harding, et al., 'Handover of Evidence Condemned', *Financial Times*, 29 November 2002, p. 8.

25 See IISS, 'Indonesia's Terrorism Links', *Strategic Comments*, vol. 8, issue 4, May 2002.

26 See generally John McBeth, 'In Search of Justice', *Far Eastern Economic Review*, pp. 20–22.

27 Fifteen local Muslims were quickly arrested, another 21 in August 2002. The Philippines followed up this success with arrests of five suspected members of the group, including Fathur Rahman al-Ghozi, an Indonesian suspected of being a regional intermediary for al-Qaeda, and the seizure of explosives apparently intended for the Singaporean terrorists. In the same time frame, the Malaysian authorities detained 23 militants belonging to a group, Kumpulan Mujahideen Malaysia (KMM, or 'Malaysian Holy Warriors' Group') connected to JI, for which they had secured large quantities of explosives.

28 The Bali bombing has produced considerable official soul-searching in European and Australian intelligence and warning circles. It transpired that the CIA,

through signals intelligence intercepts in September 2002 and June and September interrogations of Omar al-Faruq, had picked up vague indications of an impending terrorist operation against a tourist destination in Indonesia, and communicated this to other intelligence agencies, specifically mentioning Bali among 'five or six resorts'. Furthermore, the US embassy in Jakarta issued travel notices on 26 September and 10 October warning Americans and other Westerners to 'avoid large gatherings and locations known to cater primarily Western clientele, such as certain bars, restaurants and tourist areas'. Neither Australia nor the UK changes their travel advisories for Indonesia. Although both Australian Prime Minister John Howard and Downing Street insisted that the CIA warnings were too general to justify more targeted alerts, former intelligence officials from each country were considerably less sanguine. See, e.g., Alan Judd, 'To Be Forewarned Is Not To Be Forearmed', *Sunday Telegraph*, 20 October 2002, p. 26; Mark Riley, et al., 'Why Didn't They Tell Us What They Knew?', *Sydney Morning Herald*, 19 October 2002, p. 5.

29 As of early 2003, Singapore's official position was both entrenched and starkly ominous. The Ministry of Home Affairs' White Paper stated: '[T]errorism is not a new phenomenon in the region. Militant self-proclaimed Islamic terrorist groups have long existed in the region, with many espousing a separatist Islamic agenda. In addition to these indigenous groups, terrorist groups from outside the region have used Southeast Asia as a safe haven and for transit points and procurement sites ... Because of their links with Al-Qaeda, the regional

groups have become more radical and extreme in their ideology, methods and capabilities. They have also blended Al-Qaeda's agenda of global jihad against Americans and other enemies of Islam into their own local agendas'. Ministry of Home Affairs, Republic of Singapore, White Paper, 'The Jemaah Islamiyah Arrests and the Threat of Terrorism', 7 January 2003, p. 3.

30 See Jonathan M. Winer and Trifin J. Roule, 'Fighting Terrorist Finance', *Survival*, vol. 44, no. 3, autumn 2002, pp. 87–104.

31 See Kimberley L. Thachuk, 'Terrorism's Financial Lifeline: Can it be Severed?', *Strategic Forum*, no. 191, May 2002, p. 7.

32 US General Accounting Office, Terrorist Financing: U.S. Agencies Should Systematically Assess Terrorists' Use of Alternative Financing Mechanisms, www.gao.gov/new.items/d04163.pdf, November 2003, p. 24.

33 Ibid., p. 10. See also, e.g., 'West Africa: Mixed News', *Strategic Survey* 2001/2002 (Oxford: Oxford University Press for the IISS, 2002), pp. 346–48.

34 Muslims are expected to donate 2.5% of their net revenue to charity – a practice known as 'zakat'. See *Terrorist Financing: Report of an Independent Task Force Sponsored by the Council on Foreign Relations* (New York: Council on Foreign Relations, October 2002), p. 7. While devout Muslims may be the steadiest and most generous donors, many less pious ones also give significant amounts to charity to keep up appearances.

35 See Brian Bennett, 'Wahhabism: Money Trail', *Time* (Asian edition), 10 March 2003; Jeff Gerth and Judith Miller, 'Threats and Responses: The Money Trail', *New York Times*, 28 November 2003.

36 Hambali reportedly claimed, under interrogation, that JI was in dire financial shape in October 2003. Any such claim should obviously be treated with circumspection. See 'JI Near Collapse, Says Hambali', *Agence France-Presse*, 8 October 2003.

37 See Zachary Abuza, 'Funding Terrorism in Southeast Asia: The Financial Network of Al Qaeda and Jemaah Islamiya', *Contemporary Southeast Asia*, vol. 25, no. 2, August 2003, pp. 169–99.

38 The World Bank and the International Monetary Fund, 'Informal Funds Transfer Systems: An Analysis of the Hawala System', 18 December 2002.

39 See, e.g., N.S. Jamwal, 'Hawala – The Invisible Financing System of Terrorism', *Strategic Analysis*, vol. 26, no. 2, April–June 2002, pp. 188–92.

40 'Funding Terrorism in Southeast Asia', pp. 175–77.

41 Matthew Levitt, 'Stemming the Flow of Terrorist Financing: Practical and Conceptual Challenges', *Fletcher Forum of World Affairs*, vol. 27, no. 1, Winter/Spring 2003, p. 62.

42 See 'Al-Qaeda Operations are Rather Cheap', *Economist*, 4 October 2003.

43 Terrorist Financing, CFR, pp. 23, 28–29.

44 Levitt, 'Stemming the Flow', p. 64.

45 See Matthew Levitt, 'Turning a Blind Eye to Hamas in London', *Wall Street Journal Europe*, 20 October 2003.

46 See, for example, Douglas Farah, 'Al Qaeda's Finances Ample, Say Probers', *Washington Post*, 14 December 2003, p. A1.

47 Ibid., p. 26. In its second report in June 2004, the CFR Task Force criticised the executive branch for declining to take this advice. See Update on the Global Campaign Against Terrorist Financing: Second Report of an Independent Task Force on terrorist Financing (New York: Council on Foreign Relations, October 2002), p. 25.

Chapter 3

[1] Steven A. Camarota, *The Open Door: How Militant Islamic Terrorists Entered and Remained in the United States, 1993–2001* (Washington DC: Center for Immigration Studies, 2002), p. 5.

[2] 'Assimilation' is the minority's acceptance of the majority's political principles and culture; 'integration' the majority's political and cultural acceptance of the minority.

[3] See Uwe Siemon-Neto, 'France and Faith – Arcane Twist', *Washington Times*, 25 February 2003.

[4] See, e.g., Humayun Ansari, Muslims in Britain (Minority Rights Group International, 2002), pp. 9–11; 'The Situation of Muslims in France', in *Monitoring the EU Accession Process: Minority Protection* (Open Society Institute, 2002), pp. 95, 127.

[5] Olivier Roy, 'EuroIslam: The Jihad Within?', *The National Interest*, no. 71, spring 2003, pp. 63–73. Potentially amplifying the problem is an increase in converts to Islam in Europe, though most do not appear to be radical or fundamentalist. See, e.g., Craig S. Smith, 'Where the Moors Held Sway, Allah Is Praised Again', *New York Times*, 21 October 2003.

[6] See, e.g., Patrick E. Tyler and Don Van Natta Jr., 'Militants in Europe Openly Call for Jihad and the Rule of Islam', *New York Times*, 26 April 2004.

[7] Deobandis, however, are not traditionally jihadists. But in Pakistan, free from the threat of non-Muslim influences, they became more aggressive about spreading their strict brand of Islam and were politicised in the 1980s. From the 1990s, they received support from Saudi Arabia, mainly to stem Shi'ite encroachment in Central and South Asia. Not until Afghans educated in Saudi Wahhabi-supported Deobandi madrassas in Pakistan formed the Taliban, however, did Deobandism become associated with large-scale religious violence. See Gilles Kepel, *Jihad: The Trail of Political Islam* (London: I.B. Tauris & Co. Ltd., 2002), pp. 223–27. At the same time, the advent of the Taliban and its alliance with al-Qaeda gave Deobandis everywhere an opportunity to express religious fervour and political and socio-economic dissatisfaction through violence. An estimated 3,000 British Muslims trained in al-Qaeda camps in Afghanistan.

[8] Although the Arab al-Qaeda cell that perpetrated the 11 September attacks famously used Hamburg as a base, the radicalisation of indigenous German Muslims is not a major problem because most of them originate from Turkey – on the whole, a singularly secular and moderate Islamic country.

[9] Sarah Turnbull, *Almost French: A New Life in Paris* (London: Bantam Books, 2002), p. 278.

[10] Ibid., p. 279.

[11] One of the more vivid national examples is Germany's abandonment, in 1999, of its jus sanguinis ('blood right') basis of citizenship in favour of civic naturalisation and jus soli ('territorial right') rules for children of immigrants born in Germany.

[12] See, e.g., Elaine Ganley, 'France Targets Imams to Rein in Terrorism', Associated Press, 3 May 2004.

[13] See generally Daniel Benjamin and Steven Simon, 'A Place at the Table', *Time*, 16 December 2002; Jonathan Stevenson, 'Britain's New Terrorism Problem', *Wall Street Journal Europe*, 15 November 2001; Jonathan Stevenson, 'The Qaeda Vipers in

Europe's Bosom', *New York Times*, 1 February 2003.

[14] Known as 'positive discrimination' in Europe, affirmative action is technically illegal in the UK. But because Northern Irish Catholics avail themselves so readily of the thoroughgoing fair employment laws, and the Fair Employment Commission there is so attuned to the political sensitivities of the workplace, the fair employment laws have had the effect of an affirmative action policy. Note that those laws were enacted specifically with an eye towards improving ground-level conditions for Catholics in order to defuse the political conflict – and diminish terrorism – in Northern Ireland.

[15] See Jytte Klausen, 'Is There an Imam Problem?', *Prospect*, May 2004, pp. 44–46.

[16] For good reasons, this was considered unlikely before the collapse of the Oslo process and 11 September. See Philip H. Gordon, *The Transatlantic Allies and the Changing Middle East*, Adelphi Paper 322 (Oxford: Oxford University Press for the IISS, 1998). Now, it may be more feasible.

[17] Roula Khalaf, 'Media Perspectives on Public Opinion and the New Security Challenges', paper presented at the IISS Global Strategic Review, September 2003.

[18] See IISS, 'Transnational Terrorism After the Iraq War', *Strategic Comments*, vol. 9, issue 4, June 2003.

[19] Khalaf, 'Media Perspectives'.

[20] Steven R. Weisman, 'U.S. Must Counteract Image in Muslim World, Panel Says', *New York Times*, 1 October 2003.

[21] Jeffrey Gedmin and Craig Kennedy, 'Selling America – Short', *The National Interest*, no. 74, winter 2003/04, p. 74.

[22] See generally Antony Blinken, 'Winning the War of Ideas', in Alexander T.J. Lennon (ed.), *The Battle for Hearts and Minds: Using Soft Power to Undermine Terrorist Networks* (Cambridge, MA: The MIT Press, 2003), pp. 282–98.

[23] See, e.g., Amy Hawthorne, 'Middle East Democracy: Is Civil Society the Answer?', *Carnegie Paper No. 44*, March 2004.

[24] See John Waterbury, 'Hate Your Policies, Love Your Institutions', *Foreign Affairs*, vol. 82, no. 1, January/February 2003, pp. 61–62, 88–68.

[25] Kathleen M Moore, 'Open House: Visibility, Knowledge and Integration of Muslims in the United States', in Strum and Tarantolo, *Muslims in the United States*, pp. 63–77.

[26] See Jack Miles, 'Religion and American Foreign Policy', *Survival*, vol. 46, no. 1, spring 2004.

[27] See Benjamin and Simon, *The Age of Sacred Terror*, pp. 208–11.

[28] See IISS, 'Somalia and the "War" on Terrorism', *Strategic Comments*, vol. 8, issue 1, January 2002.

[29] See generally Jeffrey Herbst and Greg Mills, The Future of Africa: A New Order in Sight?, *Adelphi Paper* 361 (Oxford: Oxford University Press for the IISS, 2004), pp. 49–64.

[30] See, e.g., Jonathan Stevenson, 'Counter-terrorism and the Role of the International Financial Institutions', *Journal of Conflict, Security & Development*, vol. 1, no. 3, 2001, pp. 157–58.

[31] See 'US and the Middle East After 11 September', *Strategic Survey* 2001/2002 (Oxford: Oxford University Press for the IISS, 2002), pp. 192–96; IISS, 'US Policy Towards the Middle East', *Strategic Comments*, vol. 9, issue 1, January 2003. For a slightly more optimistic view with respect to democracy promotion – but one that remains sceptical about the democratisation potential of regime-change in Iraq – see

Thomas Carothers, 'Promoting Democracy and Fighting Terror', *Foreign Affairs*, vol. 82, no. 1, January/February 2003, pp. 84–94.

[32] See generally Jonathan Stevenson, *Preventing Conflict: The Role of the Bretton Woods Institutions*, Adelphi Paper 336 (Oxford: Oxford University Press for the IISS, 2000), pp. 18–22.

Chapter 4

[1] Thomas C. Schelling appears to have been the first to pinpoint this fallacy as such. See Thomas C, Schelling, Foreword to Roberta Wohlstetter, *Pearl Harbor: Warning and Decision* (Stanford, CA: Stanford University Press, 1962), p. vii.

[2] Dennis M. Gormley, 'Enriching Expectations: 11 September's Lessons for Missile Defence', *Survival*, vol. 44, no. 2, summer 2002, pp. 19–35. See also Philip Bobbitt, 'Seeing the Futures', *New York Times*, 8 December 2003, p. A29.

[3] Contrary to its popular image as an 'at all costs' effort that claimed resources from other priorities, the Manhattan Project was not expensive. The construction of four nuclear weapons cost a total of $20bn (in constant 1996 dollars) – less than 1% of total war costs estimated at $2.2 trillion.

[4] See, e.g., Patrick Seale, 'A Costly Friendship,' *The Nation*, July 21, 2003

[5] See, e.g., Danielle Pletka, 'Arabs on the Verge of Democracy,' *New York Times*, August 9, 2004, p. A15.

[6] 'National Strategy to Combat Weapons of Mass Destruction,' *National Security Presidential Directive 17*.

[7] John Parachini, 'Putting WMD Terrorism Into Perspective', *The Washington Quarterly*, vol. 26, no. 4, autumn 2003, pp. 37–50.

[8] Parachini, 'Putting WMD Terrorism Into Perspective,' p. 43. Along similar lines, see Jason Burke, 'Think Again: Al Qaeda', *Foreign Policy*, May/June 2004, p. 24.

[9] *Symposium: Diagnosing Al Qaeda*, 18 August 2003, http://www.rand.org/news/fp.html, p. 6.

[10] Ibid., p. 5.

[11] Ibid., p. 10. See also Paul K. Davis and Brian Michael Jenkins, 'The Influence Component of Counterterrorism', *RAND Review*, Spring 2003, pp. 12–15.

[12] Steven Simon of the RAND Corporation articulated this line of thought to the author.

[13] See generally Robert F. Trager and Dessie P. Zagorcheva, 'Countering Global Terrorism: Why the Death of Deterrence Has Been Exaggerated', paper presented at the 2003 Annual Meeting of the American Political Science Association, 28–31 August 2003.

[14] See Glenn H. Snyder, *Deterrence and Defence: Toward a Theory of National Security* (Princeton, NJ: Princeton University Press, 1961).

[15] I am indebted to Gareth Jenkins for illuminating these points.

[16] See Thomas C. Schelling, *The Strategy of Conflict* (Cambridge, MA: Harvard University Press, 1960), p. 5.

[17] See ibid., pp. 54–67.

[18] See Lawrence Freedman, *Deterrence* (Cambridge: Polity Press, 2004), pp. 127–30.

[19] See *The National Security Strategy of the United States of America*, September 2002, http://www.whitehouse.gov/nsc/nss.pdf.

[20] See Gareth Jenkins, 'Muslim Democrats in Turkey?', *Survival*, vol. 45, no. 1, spring 2003, pp. 45–66.

[21] See Karen Armstrong, *The Battle for God: Fundamentalism in Judaism, Christianity and Islam* (London: HarperCollins, 2001),

pp. 195–98, 329–33.

[22] See Ray Takeyh, 'Iran: From Reform to Revolution?', *Survival*, vol. 46, no. 1, spring 2004, p. 131.

[23] Steven Simon, 'The New Terrorism', chapter 12 in Henry J. Aaron, James M. Lindsay and Pietro S. Nivola (eds.), *Agenda for the Nation* (Washington DC: Brookings Institution Press, 2003), p. 425.

[24] See, e.g., Steven Simon and Jonathan Stevenson, 'Confronting Hamas', *The National Interest*, no. 74, winter 2003/04, pp. 59–68.

[25] Mondal, 'Liberal Islam?', p. 33.

[26] See Ray Takeyh, 'Uncle Sam in the Arab Street', *The National Interest*, no. 75, spring 2004.

[27] Mondal, 'Liberal Islam', p. 33.

[28] See, e.g., Shmuel Bar, 'The Religious Sources of Islamic Terrorism', *Policy Review*, no. 125, June & July 2004.

[29] See Miles, 'Religion and American Foreign Policy'.